Uncle Manta
and the Children of Pride

Keith Allen Hall

Illustrations by Tina Thornton

Note for Librarians: a cataloguing record for this book that includes Dewey Decimal Classification and US Library of Congress numbers is available from the Library and Archives of Canada. The complete cataloguing record can be obtained from their online database at:
www.collectionscanada.ca/amicus/index-e.html
ISBN 1-4120-3864-2
Printed in Victoria, BC, Canada

Published in Canada by Keith Allen Hall1604 - 116th AvenueDawson Creek, British Columbia, Canada V1G 3G4   ph: 250-782-8431

Produced by Donald A. Pettit Peace photoGraphicsBox 823, Dawson Creek, British Columbia, Canada V1G 4H8   ph: 250-782-6068
toll free: 1-866-373-8488   email: info@peacephotographics.com
Layout and design by Jesh de Rox, Peace photoGraphics
Illustrations by Tina Thornton

TRAFFORD

Offices in Canada, USA, Ireland, UK and Spain
This book was published *on-demand* in cooperation with Trafford Publishing. On-demand publishing is a unique process and service of making a book available for retail sale to the public taking advantage of on-demand manufacturing and Internet marketing. On-demand publishing includes promotions, retail sales, manufacturing, order fulfilment, accounting and collecting royalties on behalf of the author.
Book sales for North America and international:
Trafford Publishing, 6E–2333 Government St.,
Victoria, BC v8t 4p4 CANADA
phone 250 383 6864 (toll-free 1 888 232 4444)
fax 250 383 6804; email to orders@trafford.com
Book sales in Europe:
Trafford Publishing (uk) Ltd., Enterprise House, Wistaston Road Business Centre, Wistaston Road, Crewe, Cheshire cw2 7rp UNITED KINGDOM
phone 01270 251 396 (local rate 0845 230 9601)
facsimile 01270 254 983; orders.uk@trafford.com
Order online at:
www.trafford.com/robots/04-1672.html

10 9 8 7 6 5 4 3 2

ACKNOWLEDGEMENTS

To my wife and family who encouraged me to continue. To Larry and Diedra who shared their skill in the editing and art work. To Tina, who's illustrations captured the soul behind the words, as only a true artist could do. To Mrs. Helene Brown, who taught us that no matter what your colour, if you want it bad enough you can have it. To all my sisters and brothers, who remain in the fondest memories of my boyhood.

FORWARD

This is a story of courage, perseverance and faith. It is told in a language that provides a direct connection to the characters themselves, as well as their emotions and experiences. This adds a sense of authenticity, purity and charm to a compelling story.

This is also a story of observation. The images are rich and powerful and real . . . the reader is able to very quickly experience the events of the story, using all the senses of touch, taste, smell, sight and hearing. In short, the words place you there, an effect so rarely achieved.

The images and pictures created by these words indicate that this story could easily be transformed into a screenplay of invaluable importance. It is also the "right stuff" for a traditional childrens' adventure classic or a spiritual book of faith, as the story is compelling to all ages.

There is strength in this material. Its charm is its simplicity and its simplicity is its charm.

Larry N. Austman

Dedicated to the memory of
my parents, Grizilda and Curtis Hall
and to Mama Isy,
who encouraged me to listen and learn
no matter how incredible the story.

Uncle Manta

and the Children of Pride

PROLOGUE

Sometimes I feel like a motherless child,
A long ways from home,
Sometimes I feel like a motherless child,
A long ways from home,
True believer, a long ways from home.

The silence of the night was broken by the cry of a newborn baby, who awakened five angels of motherhood coming to the aid of yet another soul, bearing her first-born into slavery.

It was a cold November morning believed to be around 1854. The dew hung low over the Georgian bayou, the smell of freshly dug potatoes perfumed by the perspiration secreted from the six families huddled in a loft of an old wind-worn barn.

Nelly Kumo, now renamed Grant, her slave name by the master of the house, looked down upon her infant and wondered aloud what God had in store for him. She was consoled by an elder who told her that only God knew what was best and said "De boy looks like a manta." Thus from that day forward the boy was to be called "Manta", meaning teacher. The morning light brought no changes in the life of Nelly Grant, except for the private showing of her child to a few of the curious and receiving but a few small gifts of food and helpful tips on how to bring up the boy. The day began as usual, so wrapping the child in a burlap sack and lashing him across her back, she headed toward the fields with a hundred others. There they performed the laborious task of digging potatoes. Nelly had but three rest periods in that day. When the water boy finally came she gulped down her meager share, so that she could allow her child to suckle on her breast for a few minutes, to sustain him on his first day into a life of slavery.

Her day began at sunrise and ended at sunset, when weary and worn she would feed her child and change his scanty garments which could only be done once a day.

The meager rations consisted mainly of unwanted potatoes, mustard greens, and a slab of meat, which was usually thought to be either mule, rabbit, or chicken.

The father, nicknamed Robe, worked in the bayou and was away at times with several other so-called bad niggers, to cut trees from the bayou. They were always accompanied by three or four armed whites who were determined to destroy anyone who dared to step out of line. This, combined with the terrible misfortune of having a job considered to be the worst on the plantation, meant that they were away from the comforts of a warm bed. They were forced to combat waves of unbearable heat and endless hordes of mosquitoes. Many a slave did not return, not because he necessarily stepped out of line, but due to the fact that according to their charges they were just the bad niggers anyway, so who would care.

It was about four months after the birth of Manta when Nelly received the news that Robe would not return. It was said that he had died of fever. That night the families celebrated with song the crossing over of yet another soul. They believed that God in his mercy saw fit to take him home. Nelly's tears were soon over, with the realization that this was her lot in life, as she had seen many a good man die in her sixteen years in bondage. Spirited also by the fact that she now had to raise a child in such a god-forsaken place as this, she longed for the day that she too would be delivered, as Moses delivered the children of Israel out of slavery.

CHAPTER 1

Lord how come me here
Lord how come me here
They treat me so mean Lord
I wish I never was born.

The Escape

It was three, maybe four years following Robe's death, when the most important changes to be remembered in Nelly's life occurred. The slaves were moved from the barn into six by eight foot shacks, built for them out of old, rejected and weather-beaten boards, the only luxury being that of a wildflower that Nelly gathered on her way back from the fields. Nelly's most exciting change was her first pair of old shoes, given to her by a slave lady who worked as a maid in the big house. She had recovered the shoes, which bore scars of great usage and displayed large holes in each sole, from the garbage pit. Still, Nelly cherished them, as those were her very first pair of shoes in her now twenty years of life. The slaves were allowed to gather only once a week, on Sundays, and it was then that Nelly would wear her lovely shoes.

During this year, a noise was going around about a woman deliverer who was taking slaves from the plantations and walking them out of Georgia, even up to a place called Canada. It was a hot night, believed to be in July, when Nelly overheard Isaac - who was considered to be the oldest and wisest of all the slaves - reporting some gossip that he had heard. The subject was the black lady who used to be a slave, who had stolen ten slaves right out from under their plantation owners' noses, just twelve miles down the road. Isaac didn't do much work anymore, except to clean the Massa's family's shoes and saddles, but he did hear a lot about what was going on in the plantation. Nelly longed for the day that she would be lucky enough to be stolen, right out from under the Massa's nose. She laughed with delight at the thought. Her days and weeks became filled with songs like: " I got a robe, you got a robe, all God's chillun got a robe." After listening to her brothers and sisters singing those songs of deliverance, she became more obsessed with the idea that this great fortune would happen to her.

It was not too long after this that Nelly's dream appeared to be unfolding right before her very eyes. One night she heard some of the young men talking about escaping. The plan appeared to be genuine, with the added enticement that someone was to meet them in the bayou.

Excited by the half of the story that she had heard, Nelly prepared herself and her son in readiness for her great escape. Leaving her candle lit, she fled the house and hid with her child near a shed, where she knew the men would have to pass if they were going to escape. She waited for hours. Finally she heard them silently pass, then waited until they were well ahead as she feared that if her presence was detected, they would not allow her to go with them, especially with the child in her arms. She followed them fearful that she might be noticed, for what seemed to be hours even though the bayou was only a twenty minute walk past the fields. As she stumbled through the swamps, Nelly prayed constantly that little Manta would not cry.

When the men arrived at the meeting place, Nelly still did not reveal herself; keeping the mosquitoes off her child as best she could, she waited.

It was quite awhile before she heard a stirring in the trees, which caused her heart to jump with excitement and fear because she also knew it could be the slave catchers.

Nelly was too far away to hear what was being said, but she could hear faint whispering. There was no shooting, no noises, and no folks running every which way, so Nelly was quite sure that all was well. With a little reluctance, she revealed herself, much to the young men's surprise. One of them, not being sure if the noise that he had heard was friend or foe, dashed into the bayou. After a few minutes of chastisement, Nelly was allowed to stay.

Speaking to a man who said he was sent by the deliverer, Nelly's heart lightened to think that she was going to be free. But the joy was soon struck down when the man, who called himself Big Brown, said he had rules that must be kept. There was to be no talking, no stopping for any reason and, most important, everyone's shoes had to be inspected. Nelly's heart dropped as her only shoes, which were the same ones given to her from the garbage, were exhibited for inspection. Big Brown immediately told her that she could not go as she would slow them down.

Almost immediately they left, leaving Nelly in total distress as she heard the faint sounds disappear in the distance. She rested awhile, then gathered her baby and with a broken heart, she started toward home.

Not long into her journey she felt the greatest fear ever. Hearing noises behind her, she immediately hid herself and held the child's mouth to ensure silence. Heart throbbing and eyes bulging, she waited. Minutes later she discovered that it was the boy who had run away. She called to him in silence and managed to identify herself without him dashing off again. After a few seconds of reassurance, they again continued toward home.

Nelly discovered that his name was Casey and he too was a bayou worker. The journey back was long and sad for both, but first there were other, more immediate problems that had to be faced. The biggest was how to get back before being missed, or did they already know? It was almost sunrise when they reached the field. They started across the field in great fear as there were always slaves seeking favours or high positions, who would report escapees. Sometimes it was for as little as an extra water ration per day. Their fears were unfounded and with great relief they arrived safely and unnoticed. The worst thing that happened was the embarrassment caused when Casey was caught leaving

Nelly's shack when the bull man arrived to escort them to the fields. Since Casey lived further down the plantation, they chose to play it out. There was much teasing that day from the other women, but Nelly kept her secret.

It was a bit ironic to think that Nelly's flight to freedom had been foiled because her prize shoes had holes in them, but in spite of this, Nelly still sang to herself. "I got shoes, you got shoes, all God's chillun got shoes." The song convinced her that she must have good shoes for the journey so that she would not endanger the lives of others by falling behind.

Sister Moses

The years are not remembered by number but rather that it was the year of the Great Flood. It had rained profusely for weeks and the great river banks yielded to the pressure, spilling over about two and a half feet of water, which swept many shacks, including Nelly's, into the abyss. The slaves were ordered to move. Under guard, and being allowed to take only one parcel of belongings, Nelly with her five year old on her back, joined the great procession in the march to higher ground. She also took a few potatoes and a few grains of cornmeal.

During the three day march she watched two of the elderly slaves, who were unable to go any further, yield to the pull of the waters and go to their final home. Few mourned the loss, but all in great song lifted their eyes to the heavens and sang, "Swing low, sweet chariot, coming for to carry me home." Nelly was consoled by remembering the story behind the song.

They believed that in the old days, it was said that the chieftains when they died, were laid on a raft of wood with all their worldly possessions and floated down the great river. As the raft reached the brink of the falls, an angel in a chariot swept down from the skies and took the soul home to Jesus.

When the procession arrived at their destination on the third evening, as everyone was cold and exhausted from the journey, they collapsed on the ground to rest. Not a word was heard from child nor beast for hours. Nelly, asleep with the child in her arms, was awakened quietly by one of the women who asked if she would share what little alms she had left with the others. Nelly noticed that the bull men were not around and was told that "dem not been with us for two days now." Nelly wondered how it was possible for her not to notice such a marvelous thing as that. After a meager meal, which was the end of all their provisions, everyone laid down to rest again.

The next morning Nelly arose in panic to find that Manta was missing. Her screams of terror awoke all but a few, and moments later the search began with people running in all directions looking for yet another lost soul. Nelly searched for hours in vain for the child, then started back to the main camp in hopes that someone was more fortunate in their search than she. It was hours later when she arrived and instantly sensed, without asking a word, that their efforts too were in vain. She fell on her knees and prayed and wept over her plight. She crumbled to the ground, a broken soul, and fell asleep. When she awoke the expressions on the faces of her colleagues told her that Manta had not been found.

To many this was just another soul, who was lost in the wilderness, in the hands of his Maker. The conversation soon changed from the child to more important problems, namely food and shelter, which must be overcome quickly if they were to survive this new chapter in the episode of their lives. Some of the elderly among them suggested that they should all pray and sing for forgiveness and maybe if Jesus was awake, he might just stop the rain. It rained all night

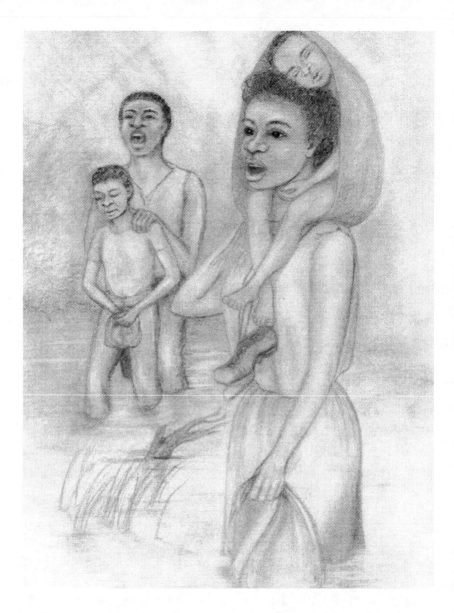

without a break until just before dawn, and when Nelly awoke she could see rays of sunlight through the thick trees. She wondered once again about the plight of her child, then the silence was broken by the rustle of wet leaves beside her. Nelly looked down and saw a brown squirrel playing nearby and noticed that it clasped a bright red berry in it's paws.

She reached out for the berry in the hope that the squirrel would surrender it to her. The squirrel fled in fear into the thicket and Nelly decided to follow. She hoped to find a tree that might provide food, but as she broke through the thick bush she saw instead, haloed in light in the near distance, a child with out-stretched arms. Having to shade her eyes from the sun's glare, Nelly realized that her prayers had been answered, for before her stood Manta. With a shout of joy she embraced her child, but Manta said not a word.

The search for food began, and scattered in all directions were a hundred or so treasure seekers in search of the most precious of treasures, food. It was about noon of that day that Nelly noticed that Manta had not uttered a single word and she wondered if he was ill. When Nelly arrived back at the camp, she discovered that no one had found a morsel of food and all was again quiet for several hours. Nelly's combination of discouragement and excitement forced her to forget the squirrel that she had noticed earlier. She laid down in an attempt to rest, when Manta touched her shoulder and uttered his first words of the day, "Come with me." When Nelly reached out to him, he quickly backed away. Nelly was too tired to want to go anywhere and she tried to reach him once again, but he eluded her and repeated, "Come with me."

Reluctantly she rose to her feet and followed him for another hour, then suddenly they came upon the most splendid gift she could ever hope for. Nestled in the thicket were trees loaded with beautiful red berries, so grabbing an handful she raced toward the main camp to show her rewards, with Manta running close behind.

The people were overjoyed to see such a welcome sight, and after a quick explanation as to how she had discovered the berries, all but the elderly headed towards the treasure. When Nelly arrived, there were many people recklessly grabbing fruit, branches and anything that looked edible. One young man even uprooted a complete bush. The trees were quickly being depleted of all the fruit, when above all of the noise of excitement there came the loud cry of a child. He shouted, "Stop, stop!" Most people did so just to see why they should. It was Manta, who quickly defended the trees with his body and with out-stretched arms he said, "You must not break the trees, only eat the big berries and eat enough to feed yourselves. If you eat them all, we will have no more and we will die."

Most people seemed to understand and selected their fruit with caution, while others decided that if these were here there must be others. Manta replied, "There are no others." This statement drew the attention of all as they watched this youngster who was still shielding the berry bushes. In awe, the people stopped and headed up the hill quietly. Nelly looked at her child in amazement and began to wonder if such a miraculous thing could have actually happened to her son.

On her journey back towards the camp, she wondered whether the silence from the people meant that they were angry or if they believed what Manta had said. Soon she could hear voices raised in praise and the people finished the last half of the walk singing. "Didn't My Lord Deliver Daniel?" Nelly hummed the Negro spiritual silently with them. She began to notice that the day's events had lightened the hearts of many and it was not long before everyone was constructing some sort of shelter. Wood was also gathered to be burned for the night's warmth.

During the night, as the fire died down, Nelly looked upon the face of her child and wondered anew what was in store for him.

It was two days hence when Nelly was awakened with many others by an unusual silence. The normal noises of the forest had ceased and the quietness of the moment had aroused them from their sleep. Manta was already sitting in silence nearby, when suddenly from outside of the encampment of bodies, stood a lady and two men. One was a white man.

The lady was dressed in darkness and it appeared that

16

she had camouflaged her face with coal which made her already dark face even darker. The other man, a slave, led her to a place of rest on a nearby felled tree. The white man was attired in what appeared to be an old suit with many missing buttons. He sat down in an exhausted fashion with his arms on his knees and head lunged forward between them. Moments passed before a word was spoken.

Breaking the silence of the moment was the voice of a child who quavered "Mama Moses?"

The black lady raised her head and answered, "Yes child, it is me." The congregation was amazed to find that Manta knew this lady's name, for this was the lady that they had heard about, but no one had ever met. There were even a few who doubted her existence.

Isaac, who had miraculously survived the flood, was the first to speak up. "You de lady Moses we's all hear about?"

"Yes," she replied. "We were passing by when we noticed you and, with the Lord's help, we will take you with us."

Nelly was the first to leap to her feet. "Praise de Lord," she shouted and immediately grabbed Manta by the hands and started to dance around him. She shouted, "I got my shoes. I got my shoes." Isaac motioned her to sit down, which she did immediately. "But we be a hundred or more, how we do dat widout been seen?"

Isaac explained, "We must take only twenty at a time."

Mama Moses explained, "And you all must move from here, the rain is over and soon you will be found."

"Dey knows we are here, dey brong us here," cried Isaac.

"Then we must move fast, we'll move up river, then go twenty at a time," she replied.

He's got the whole world in His hands –
He's got you and me, brother, in His hands –
He's got you and me, sister, in His hands –
He's got the fish in the sea in His hands –
He's got everybody in His hands –
He's got the little bitty baby in His hands –
He's got the whole world in His hands.

CHAPTER 2

The Chosen Few

Within minutes the entire congregation was on its way, but with the utmost silence. A few minutes later they met the remainder of Mama Moses' group, a small gathering of slaves, about fifteen in all - ill fed and exhausted. Nelly marched hurriedly along beside Mama Moses, with one hand clutching the hand of her child and the other carrying her prize shoes. They marched throughout the day and night without a stop. Mama Moses constantly assured them that God was watching over them and told them that they all must help the elderly to catch up.

They finally stopped the following day near noon. Here Mama Moses told them that they must split up into groups of twenty, then break away from each other for at least a half day's walk. This, she assured them, would prevent the slave catchers from catching the entire group together.

Nelly's heart thumped with excitement at the thought of being one of the first lucky twenty chosen to go on this trip. Much to her dismay, Mama Moses did not make the selection herself. The white man with the beard stood up, and Nelly being over anxious, stood as he did. He looked for a second at the child standing beside her then quickly looked the other way.

Pointing to the crowd he said, "You, you, you, and you." The hope in Nelly's heart dwindled with every "you" he uttered and soon the selection was over. Nelly was not among them and sadly she fell to the ground still holding Manta's hand. In an hour or so she joined one of the groups led by Isaac, as she respected his judgment and age. They continued for yet another half day's walk to the north, with

Isaac constantly stopping to rest his callused feet and to check the bottoms of the trees for moss, as he felt that this was the best way to find north.

The sun was setting when finally they stopped, and exhausted, they laid down among the trees. No fires were to be built and no one appeared to be hungry, so within minutes, all were asleep.

Sunrise came early and once again a panic-stricken cry from Nelly awoke the small company - Manta had wandered off again. Isaac motioned her to be quiet and then everyone set out to search. It did not take long however, and Isaac soon found the small boy about a quarter of a mile away. Manta was facing the sun on his knees and appeared to be in prayer. When asked why he had wandered off, there was no reply.

Upon Isaac's return, Nelly was in tears and in her frustration, she slapped Manta across the face bringing not a tear to his eyes. Still with no explanation as to why he had run off, he put his hand under his shirt and pulled out a handful of red berries. The anxiety quickly lightened and a few hurried promptings encouraged the group to go where the bushes were. With great joy they ate their fill, this time they only ate the big ones and not a branch was broken. Old Isaac hummed himself to sleep with a spiritual while the others continued to look for other edible things.

Nelly laid down again and quietly stared at her child, wondering once again, what would become of him.

A week or more passed and their prayers were not answered as there was no sign of Mama Moses. The people grew restless and one man and his wife questioned if she would ever return for them. Worse still, fear of the consequences, which they would face if they were ever caught, was thrown into the hearts of all. No one commented at all on the statements made, but they laid there as though frozen with apprehension about their plight. What would tomorrow bring?

Days passed and still no sign was evident, but early

one morning Manta woke everyone in the party and whispered that they must move now. He told them that Jesus had told him to tell them that they must move, NOW!!

Nelly hushed him quickly and Isaac questioned him as to how he knew that they must move. Manta repeated "Now! Now!", and broke from his mother's hand and ran into the woods. Nelly ran after him and Isaac gestured to the people to come, however all but four people remained. They were but a short distance away when screams of horror swept over them. Frozen in their tracks, they listened to the sound of gunshots and horses' hooves. The party of four hid until the noises had ceased and then came the realization that horror had descended upon the non-believers.

Their fears were soon confirmed when, within minutes after the sounds had ceased, Manta broke away from his mother and rushed to the scene of the massacre. All those who had remained were dead. The four survivors fell on their knees in prayer. It was Manta who interrupted by saying, "We now must go that way," pointing east. This time no one doubted his word and taking the boy, one on each hand, they headed in the direction that Isaac thought was east.

Their journey continued for two days without stopping to eat or rest. They did encounter edible hard berries at times and grabbing quick handfuls, they continued. On the second night Nelly pleaded with Isaac to take the child and leave her, as she would only slow them down. Her feet were bleeding and torn, preventing her from going any further.

Manta instantly refused the proposal and said that they had come far enough east and that they must turn north again. Hungry and exhausted, they rested once again as the terrain was almost impassable. Isaac sat for a few minutes and was soon fast asleep. Nelly nursed her swollen feet as best she could by placing them into a puddle of muddy water, after being instructed to do so by Manta. Her feet hurt so bad that she did not question Manta's instructions and she soon found that the treatment did bring some relief.

Manta told the others that he was going to search for food. No one questioned him. Nelly could not have followed him even if she did disapprove. About an hour later Manta returned with a shirt full of berries and four or five ears of corn. After devouring the corn, the juicy berries provided much needed moisture to their parched throats. That night, the air was filled with the smell of clover. They could hear the familiar vocalizations of wolves and wild dogs. Huddling together, the serenity of sleep soon overcame them and then all was quiet.

It was just about dawn when Nelly was shaken by her son, who gave her four ears of corn and told her to wake the others as they had to move. After giving the others equal shares of the corn, they left immediately towards the north. Soon they came to the edge of a field which told them where the corn had come from. In the distance they could see smoke billowing from a chimney of a stately built log cabin. Staying close to the edge of the field, they travelled the circumference until it was far behind them. Old Isaac was feeling a little more secure and started to hum quietly the strains of those wonderful songs of yearning which dwelt in the hearts of all slaves.

Nelly's feet appeared to be better but they were still swollen too large for her prize shoes to adorn her sore feet. Isaac was weary after a good day's journey so he laid down to rest without a sound. The others slept also, using their small bag of worldly possessions for a pillow. The girl with them was Bertha Samuel, who was about two or three years older than Manta. She said very little but Nelly remembered how it was not too long ago when she had tried to render a song through the expression of whistling. Nelly smiled when she envisioned little Bertha's mouth, puckered and blowing, without a single sound being produced. She thought of the frustration she had seen on the little girl's face when, try as she might, she still could not do it. She also remembered the jubilation that arose on the day that Bertha had whistled her first note. Nelly smiled almost with laughter to think that until now Bertha had never stopped whistling and little could be done to stop her. She began to wonder if Bertha would ever whistle again, being that her mother and father had been among the sixteen killed by the slave catchers only a week before.

After four more days of hard journey had passed, old Isaac complained of pains in his chest and Nelly saw the anguish on his face with every step. On this day, Manta told them that this was where they must stay and told them that they would be safe. After making Isaac as comfortable as possible, Nelly searched the woods for food. Being very weak herself, she stumbled about in the search but found nothing, except for the abundance of water as she rested on the bank of a slow-running stream.

Nelly was becoming more and more distressed with her plight and began to doubt that this little child had the ability to know which way they should be going. Awakening Isaac, whom she had grown to love, she asked him why he believed that Manta was right. To her surprise, he answered her by saying, "Child, that boy of yourn was chosen to lead us out of de wilderness. I will not be long in dis worl', he know dat I be free before dis night is over." Without another word, Isaac slipped back into sleep.

Bertha and Manta appeared to be playing in the soft earth on the stream bank and Nelly, being totally exhausted, was consoled that they at least had something to do to occupy their time. Darkness crept over the land and with it the sword of death. Isaac died in his sleep. Nelly tried to awaken him but could not generate any movement. She fell to her knees and cried out loud, "Oh God, what we do now, which way is north?"

Manta came to her side and tried to secure some peace in Nelly's heart by saying, "He's gone home with Jesus. Let's bury him." Nelly avoided his words of comfort and wept heartbroken for quite awhile. When Manta asked for her help to move him, she glanced down for the first time that day towards the bank of the stream and realized to her surprise, that Manta had known yesterday that Old Isaac was about to die. She saw that while Manta was playing in the sand, he had dug a grave.

After trying to console herself with the realization that, in fact, they were not alone, she remembered what old Isaac had told her just the day before and concluded that Manta was, indeed, chosen to lead them out of the wilderness. She struggled with the help of the children to put Isaac into the hole. His weight being too much for them,

24

resulted in Isaac falling face down into the shallow dug out. Even with all of their attempts to turn him over, the task was too great, and Isaac ended up being buried face down. Nelly's anxiety was great; however, the feeble trio covered the body with the dew moistened ground.

With great sadness and fear, Nelly motioned the children to leave the grave site. After glancing back momentarily while gathering their meager belongings, they immediately started out once again.

The Feast

For many days they wandered in the wilderness. Nelly could not help but remember the story she had heard of the children of Israel, who had wandered in the wilderness for forty years because they had disobeyed God's laws.

She wondered if their journey would ever end and she constantly thought of the plantation and her little hut, which now seemed to be like a castle. In her tired mind, she surmised that all must not be right with her and her God or she would not be facing the hardships that were constantly her lot.

Nelly grew more aware that the nights were getting colder, which was evident by the morning dew which often laid as crystals on the ground. She knew that winter was near. The berries were getting hard to find and the ones that they did find were already rotten and laying on the ground.

It was a cold, late autumn morning when the bawl of cattle could be heard in the distance. Fearing for the safety of the children, Nelly quickly led them to what she thought was deeper into the woods. She discovered, too late, that she was getting closer to the source of her fears. Suddenly, to her horror, she realized that she had led the children into the path of a stranger, who was seated on the back of a horse. Nelly noticed the horse and quickly tried to blank out who she envisioned could be seated on it. Clutching the children in her arms, she knelt beside them with her eyes closed. Please Massa, please don't hurt us," she pleaded.

His laughter persuaded her to at least gaze upon his face. "Woman, what you do here?" Then Nelly looked up in a strained stare and saw a handsome black man seated on the horse.

"Are you a slave catcher?" she asked.

"No", he replied, "I'm Joseph and I run cows for Missa Johnson."

"Who's Missa Johnson?" she asked.

"Mr. Johnson, he de man who own dis land you'se standing on."

Nelly looked towards her feet and asked, "Are you a slave?"

"No mam, I is free, the Colonel give me my freedom a year or so ago. But he don't like trouble, and you is trouble."

"But the chillun are hungry." Nelly replied.

Suddenly a shuffling of branches seemed to arouse fear in Joseph, who instantly motioned her and the children to back off into the bush.

The big horse, on instant reining orders, thrust his body toward the unsuspecting threesome; forcing Nelly to fall backward to the ground, with an undignified display of legs, feet and petticoat. Anger almost gave the trespassers away, as Nelly instantly rose to her feet, fist raised in contempt. She instantly restrained Manta and quickly hid behind the foliage.

Joseph quickly thundered away, no doubt to lead his unwanted companions away from the scene.

Nelly laid still and silent with Manta clutched tightly in her arms as the sound of hooves filled her ears, sparking even greater fear in her heart. As the noises faded, Nelly hastened the children deeper into the thicket, hoping to avoid being noticed.

Nelly, though comforted by the black face she had met, also knew the danger that would result if anyone learned of her existence. Without looking back, Nelly motioned the children to hurry. Perspiration filled her eyes and fear filled her heart in such a way that all reasoning seemed to denote trouble.

Who was Joseph? Many a slave sold out a fellow brother or sister in the hope that life's burdens could be lightened. If Massa could only recognize a good nigger, reporting a runaway was probably the best way to gain that favour. Or maybe this Joseph was an evil man who just wanted a woman whom he could abuse. After all, he did have a horse and surely he had to make many a black man suffer to gain such a big favour from the Massa.

It was several hours later when Nelly's senses were aroused by the smell of food. Nelly motioned to the children to be silent. Her nostrils flared in a desperate attempt to search out the direction of the food. Her hunger aided the search by making her sense of smell even more keen, and soon all three wilderness wanderers were attuned to what appeared to be the source.

Nelly motioned the children to be quiet, but did not lead them away from what could result in a feast. She tried to reason that not even food was important enough to risk endangering the lives of the children. But if only she could discover who was responsible for the food - maybe they were friendly. They might even be slaves.

She gathered the children close to her and motioned them to sit still, without a sound, and wait until she returned. Nelly was but a few steps away when she could see a faint wisp of smoke, drifting towards her, carrying with it the pleasant scent that carried her beyond the realm of safety to explore. Soon she peered through the thick branches with unbelieving eyes for there, stooped before her, was Joseph.

"You'se hungry?" Nelly could not believe that he was talking to her, but there was no one else around. She stood behind him, how could he see her? She started to back away when the voice said again, "You'se hungry?"

Nelly, motionless, replied, "Yes sir."

"Then bring them chillun and eat, woman." Joseph

27

maneuvered to face her. Nelly, unsure of her decision, turned towards the children and discovered that they did not need to be retrieved for they had followed her.

"Come," the gruff, soft voice spoke. Almost without hesitation the children surrounded the warmth of the fire, but waited for the nod from Nelly to proceed with the long forgotten practice of eating. The instant that their stomachs were full, the children laid sound asleep around the fire. Nelly had to fight the threat of sleep, as her trust in the stranger was not as strong as the children's.

It was said that when the children awoke, Nelly lay asleep, and Joseph was nowhere to be found. Nor did they ever see him again, but Nelly would never forget the dark stranger who provided a great feast and left, and that this blessing came at a time when all seemed lost. The Master had provided once again.

Now nourished they gathered the remains of the food and the trio set out once again to find the promised land.

CHAPTER 3

The Miracle

It was a cold morning when Manta was excitedly aroused by the apparent sound of howling coyotes. The dew hung heavy around him, and through it all, he could faintly see their images. Fearing that the images could be wolves, he reached over to where his mother lay and gently placed his hand over her mouth, in hopes of muffling the ever-present wheezing sound which developed from tired lungs and unattended pneumonia. Nelly awakened and was instantly hushed by a finger held vertically against her lips. Manta motioned her not to move.

Climbing to his feet, Manta tried to see beyond the fog, in hopes of finding a suitable path of escape. To his travail, he realized that he was, in fact, surrounded by wolves. He signalled to the tired body, who lay weak on the ground, to rise in silence. Nelly was aided by the helping hand of a boy, who himself was weak with fear. The maneuver was successful.

Manta realized that if worse came to worst, it would be better to be attacked while standing. Looking around for something to hold in his hand for defence, he gazed into the ashes of last night's warmth to discover a lone cinder still aspark. He wondered if it could be rekindled into a flame without arousing unwanted trouble, which could overcome them if one mistake was made. Without thought, the boy instantly but silently, removed his torn burlap jacket and placed it on the lone, smoldering tinder. He tickled the tinder gently with his sleeve, hoping beyond hope, that the night dew had not moistened his garment beyond the point of ignition.

The silence was broken by an unwanted asthmatic

cough, which no longer could be held. Though Manta's mother had relieved the congestion in her lungs, the sound attracted the animals which drew nearer. Manta knew their presence had been discovered. A lone wolf broke through the inner circle, well chosen the evening before as a place of refuge. The walls of security tumbled as yet another beast invaded the sanctuary. Fear overcame Manta, trembling and with a rush of trepidation, he dropped the burlap coat onto the smoldering ashes and embraced his mother and helped her to keep afoot. Soon they were surrounded by growling wolves whose teeth sparkled above anything else that could be remembered.

The trio, fearing that all was lost, called upon the only lasting source of power they had and started to sing aloud the Negro spiritual, "Didn't The Lord Deliver Daniel?" The weak melodic tones soon brought the entire pack to the scene of their opponent's demise.

Within minutes they were totally surrounded. The most aggressive among them were only feet away from their prey. Suddenly, when all hope appeared to be lost, Manta's coat ignited in a great burst of flame. The smoldering ashes had claimed its fuel, thus giving off a brilliant light which silhouetted the attackers and the surrounding moisture laden air about them. The suddenness of the combustion threw fear into the hearts of the beasts, so much that they fled in all directions and once again the sanctuary was free of danger.

The two collapsed to the ground in great relief as Nelly completed the last stanza to her song. Truly, as Daniel was delivered from the lion's den, so were the three vagabonds delivered out of the hands of the enemy.

Their faith now strengthened, the group moved on in silence, so as to avoid another confrontation with the same fate.

Dusk had settled before the boy and his mother had come to an exhausted stop. Not a word was spoken between them all that day. All thirst and hunger had disappeared as did the shadows of the day. Within minutes all lay sound asleep. It was well into the next day before Manta awoke. The sun was warm on his face and his eyes sensed the salt from beads of perspiration which clung to his brow. Shaking his mother gently until she awakened assured him that a precious life had been spared to see yet another day.

Nelly, now even weaker than the day before, was helped to her knees and finally to her feet. The morning dew was moist and cool about their bodies, and with each warm breath taken and exhaled, Manta could see his breath as though he was smoking old Isaac's corn pipe. Breaking a twig from a branch and placing it between his lips comforted his imagination somewhat. Nelly, not knowing the intent, did not say a word about it and the journey continued.

The endless days of travel with meager nourishment had taken its toll. Nelly appeared to have lost half of her body weight, and the heat of the day and the coldness of the nights appeared to weaken her even more. Each day her cough grew heavier until one day she could not go any further, so she told the children to go without her.

Manta's heart and hopes grew dim with the realization that the spirit of freedom was quickly dying in God's chosen instrument, who bore him in an old barn. His mind confused and angry, he ran frantically through the woods for what seemed like hours.

Collapsed and exhausted beyond all human endurance, he pounded his hands against the ground and cried aloud. "There is no God, there is no God."

His sobs were astonishingly broken by a voice who exclaimed, "Yes child, there be a God."

The voice frightened the child so that he leaped to his feet and backed away from the image that stood before him. His vision, fogged with tears, affected his ability to focus on the image. Wiping the tears from his eyes to his cheek, he could clearly see a woman – it was not a spirit but an actual being. Still engrossed with fear, Manta looked around him to seek an avenue of escape in case this vision was, in fact, not living. "Woman, who be you? Is you real?"

"Yes, I'se real. Boy what you do here?"

Manta, still backing away, stumbled backward, falling hard on his behind which now hindered his hasty retreat if it were necessary. Manta, with eyes bulging, was sure that this had to be a dream or at the most, something evil. "What's you name, boy?"

"Manta," he shakily replied.

"What you doing here, boy?"

"My Mama. My Mama," he replied.

"What about your Mama?" was the gentle inquiry.

"She be in the woods, she is sick."

"Show me where, boy."

Manta hastened to his feet and faced his apparition in silence for a few long seconds in hopes of restraining his fears long enough to determine whether he could trust this lady who had appeared out of nowhere. Then, without a word, he turned and headed into the thicket. The woman followed. Manta often checked his distance by turning his head while in motion to see if she was still following.

They neared the spot where his mother lay. It was not difficult to pinpoint the exact location as the groans, interspersed with coughing, could easily be heard.

The woman, yet unidentified, rushed to her aid. Taking what appeared to be a small vase from under her torn burlap cloak, she quickly opened the dry, parched mouth of the woman and poured a little liquid on her tongue. Manta watched with concern as the woman removed her outer garment and placed it around his mother.

"We must keep her warm," she said, "and we must find food. There is none here."

Manta noticed that the woman's face grew despondent, and tears rolled down her cheeks. Was she crying out of sadness for his mother, or was she ill? Manta was later to discover why.

The woman's despair grew deeper and not long after, she rose to her feet and exclaimed that she must go back. "Go back to where?" wondered Manta. Surely the months of

32

journey could not be reperformed by turning back. But before he could gather a moment's thought, the woman helped his mother to stand, and with one arm around her thin waist and holding on to a brittle wrist, which she lifted over her shoulder, led her away.

Stupefied, Manta followed the slow movement of the two back down the path from which the woman and he had just travelled. Manta, though concerned for his mother's health, was pleased to see that they were not retreating. His mind flashed back to the wolves, to the slaughter, and to the burial of his old friend Isaac.

Lord how come me here
Lord how come me here
They treat me so mean Lord
I wish I never was born.

Back to Bondage

Consoled by the unknown lady's remarks that she must return, assured Manta that she must have somewhere to go back to and that maybe his mother could be helped there.

The woman tirelessly carried, sometimes had to drag, her burden for what seemed like days. By nightfall, Manta noticed that the trees were getting thinner and fewer, but the journey did not stop. Soon all of the trees were behind them and the strong odour of cottonseed perfumed the air. Manta was familiar with the smell, and knew that they were travelling through a cotton field. By now the darkness of night had consumed the light of day, so much so that Manta had difficulty placing his feet without stumbling.

Without a rest, the laborious trek continued. Arms and legs were full of minor lacerations, inflicted upon them by shrubs. Finally they came to the edge of the field. Not too far ahead of them, Manta could see the faint glimmer of lights. "Where are we going?" he thought, which was dispelled by the thought that no matter where they were going, help for his mother may be just ahead.

It wasn't long before Manta realized where this angel of mercy had led them. Yes, it was a plantation and yes, back to bondage.

In silence they came closer to the source of light, and step by laborious step, the reality of their demise grew prevalent. Voices and laughter could be heard. Familiar to Manta in such a way that it drew fear into his heart, as these were the sounds of drunken men, much like the sounds he had heard coming from the slave catcher's cabins at home.

The woman gestured Manta for added silence as they passed by the sure source of danger should they be discovered. They came upon a long barn-shaped building and without knocking they entered. Manta tried to adjust his eyes to the added darkness of the room as he could not clearly see. The reality was once again reiterated by the scent of bodies crammed into a poorly ventilated abode. Yes, they had once again been delivered back into bondage.

By the sounds in the room it was going to be very difficult to find a place to lay down, but soon a plot of ground was found and treatment began immediately.

Manta sat motionless among the sleeping bodies, afraid to move, as the immense darkness of the strange sanctuary made him uncertain as to where he could lay without arousing anyone. Blinded by the haze of darkness, Manta could sense movement rather than see it. He knew his Mama was being aided by the brethren of hope which comforted Manta a little but the laughter, which he could still hear coming from across the compound dispelled most efforts to rest.

The morning light crept through the wide cracks in the rustic structure. The condensation in the bleak atmosphere was accentuated by the rays of sun, which seemed to make the dust in the air dance among the rays, with the slightest movement of air. The crow of a rooster gave credence that yes, a new day had dawned. Manta's curiosity overcame him as he crawled closer to an opening for a chance to peek out at his new conditions of life, which enveloped his utmost feelings. Manta was once again reminded that he was indeed a slave. Manta thought for a moment about how much of a sacrifice the woman made by retrieving them to her place of bondage. Manta now understood why the woman had lamented over her return, as she too, was a runaway slave.

The quietness of the morning so ended with the second crowing of the rooster, which seemed to be the signal for all to rise. The instant response to nature's alarm shocked Manta into the reality that he was among strangers. Yet the bonds of slavery seemed to assure him that he was accepted among the brethren.

Without words, breakfast consisted of a raw potato, which was thrown at his feet in haste by a kind stranger, no doubt sacrificing a portion of his daily ration. All too soon all that remained was two scared children, a frail woman, the scent of perspiration and bundles of burlap sacks, which were used for bedding.

The ensuing weeks were filled with fear and uncertainty. Little is known of what events took place during this period of time. The name of this plantation is not known, but Manta remembered that it must have taken weeks of hiding in absolute silence before Nelly was well enough to stand. After many narrow escapes, plans were being contrived by some for their escape.

Soon after, Nelly and Manta, during the dead of night, were escorted by a man, yet unknown, through the fields once again to continue their journey of freedom.

Though her name is not known, Manta never forgot the lady who sacrificed her freedom to save the life of his mother.

Truly greater love hath no man than this, that a man

lay down his life for his friends.

The promised land was still the goal, and with renewed vigour, Nelly assured her son that the journey to find it would continue. They left in the dead of the night with a small sack of provisions. They received some last minute instructions from those who knew how to pull off the great escape, but lacked the courage to try.

Nelly and Manta, shielded in the cloak of darkness, stole away to freedom once again.

Steal away, steal away,
Steal away to Jesus.
Steal away, steal away home,
I ain't got long to stay here.

My Lord calls me,
He calls me by the thunder.
The trumpet sounds within-a my soul,
I ain't got long to stay here.

CHAPTER 4

The Blues

The healing process had taken weeks and during that time, Nelly had heard many a story. One story she had heard was that soon there was going to be a war. Some said the war had already started. It was even said that one army would be dressed in blue and the other would be in grey. Some people said the slaves would be set free.

The moon shone bright and seemed to sparkle in the dew as it rose from the ground. Nelly and the children could see the trail very clearly and decided to follow it, as Nelly felt that she could spot danger more clearly. Also, she realized that for the first time during the entire journey, this was the first road that she had walked upon. They made good time. The darkness, broken by the moonlight, cast shadows across the path, which were confusing at a distance, thus, forcing Nelly at times to flee the luxury of the road and quickly hide in the camouflage of trees or bushes on the sides, just to find that there was no danger at all.

Nelly was soon to realize that with the added distance covered in such a short time it was best that they travel by night, follow the road, and sleep by day. This plan seemed to work well for many days until one day the shelter of the trees was scarce, and they were forced to walk long distances, exposed to all possible evils that could befall them. Before each stretch, Nelly and the children stopped to pray that God would guide them across, just as God had led the children of Israel across the Red Sea. Thus she reminded the children of the story of Moses, and at every exposed stretch of road, they pretended that every open stretch was the Red Sea.

The game worked well for many days, until one day halfway across the open stretch of road, the ultimate in fear befell the group. The rumble of horses plus the sound of chains and wagons wheels, descended upon them without warning as though they had fallen out of the sky. Nelly grasped the children's hands with the mightiest of strength that she could gather. Closing her eyes, frozen in a motionless seizure, she hoped that the thundering noises she had heard were not there.

Much to her surprise, the noises thundered by. So close did they pass that Nelly could smell the bodies of horses and men. Yet they did not stop Nelly's curiosity and it overcame her. Slowly opening her eyes she saw before her many soldiers, all dressed in blue. Nelly wondered if the game that they had played had turned true. Could this be the army that Pharaoh had sent after the children of Israel?

The troops were passing them without a word, the odd soldier gestured by finger-tipping his hat to Nelly's astonishment. There were many black soldiers all dressed up with bright, shining buttons. This must be the army that everyone was talking about. As the company of men passed, Nelly was indeed relieved to know that they were unharmed, as a matter of fact, some even smiled at her. The march continued.

It was not many days later, while the trio rested in the shade of the thicket, Nelly and the children heard the sound of wagon wheels and voices. Nelly hushed the children back to sleep while she peeped through the shrubbery to see what was going on. To her surprise, there were several wagons loaded down with people. Excitement filled her heart for these people appeared to be free black people, why some were even laughing!

Nelly gave little thought to the consequences and roused the children to their feet. Grabbing the children by their hands, she led them out into the path of the slow moving wagons. Her excitement was soon squelched into horror. She stepped into view revealing her presence to all before Nelly noticed that yes, these people were black, but they were definitely not free. The wagons were filled with slaves who were chained.

A slave motioned her to go back into the cover of the thicket. Too late! Nelly and the children were captured by two men on horse back and bodily thrown onto two separate wagons. Nelly, filled with fear, said not a word, but sobbed herself to sleep. Manta comforted her by rendering words of hope that all would be well. Surely they would not be hurt, as the slave master needed good niggers who were healthy.

Fear grew heavy in Manta's heart as he watched his mother sleep. She was not at all well. Again her wheezing gave her health away. Manta softly prayed aloud that God would heal his mother, so that she would not be left behind.

Not a word was spoken by anyone, no questions asked and no answers given. It was several hours later when Nelly awoke, she soon noticed the sugar cane fields. To her horror, this plantation looked familiar. How could this be unless, after all these months, they had been travelling in circles. Like the children of Israel, they had wandered in the wilderness. Nelly had indeed been here before, when she was very young. This place drew many sad memories as well. This was the very place that Nelly's mother was called home to glory.

Finally the wagon wheels stopped. As the dust cleared, Nelly surveyed the situation with contempt. It did not take long before Nelly realized that these people had come from several plantations, though she saw no one familiar. She felt a kindred spirit among them. Fear was indeed prevalent in the eyes of all. Shackles bound all the ankles of the men and women. Only the children were allowed to run free behind their mothers, like baby lambs who needed to suckle their mothers breast. The slavers knew well that the children would follow their mothers, even into hell.

That night Nelly was shackled as well and herded with some hundred and fifty others to a place in the woods. Tents were erected for the slave drivers and guards. The slaves, however, remained unprotected. That night the silence was unbearable. Manta wished that someone would just cry to break the silence. However, no one did.

The sun rose all too quickly and soon all eyes viewed another chapter of their demise. In all there were twenty wagons. Ten held at least fifteen people. Some wagons held food supplies, mostly potatoes and raw sugar cane. Two wagons held water and to Manta's surprise, two wagons were devoted to chain shackles and to things Manta had heard people call nigger yokes.

First the people were herded into the empty wagons. Within minutes, a man dumped a bucket of raw potatoes into each wagon and a sheep skin of water with no dipper. Manta noticed that the hay in the bottom of the wagon was soiled with human waste and smelled of urine. Immediately after the wagons had pulled out, Manta noticed that some of the children preferred to run beside the wagons. Manta also watched, to his horror, as a little boy with a twisted ankle fell by the wayside. No one stopped. Manta saw the mother of the child scream with terror as her wagon travelled further and further away from her boy. She helplessly watched her child struggle to his feet in vain and fall in the path of a team of horses pulling the chain wagon. The mother uttered not another word but again sat down and stared at her feet for many hours.

The evening came without anyone being allowed to leave the wagons. The dead among them were unshackled and left on the side of the road. Everyone who was asleep was nudged with a cane to ensure that they were alive. This was mostly done to see if they were well enough to continue. One of the drivers warned that anyone who was sick would be shot. He suggested that any nigger who could not walk or work is of no value to anyone. Manta shook Nelly vigorously by pushing hard on her shoulder. "Mama, Mama," he cried in anguish, "you must stay awake." To Manta's surprise he realized that neither he nor his mother had eaten at all that day. When he searched the bottom of the wagon there was nothing to be found, not even a potato peel much less a potato. Someone in the wagon ahead of Manta started to sing, "Swing low, sweet chariot, coming for to carry me home." The snap of a whip and an agonized cry immediately ended the soulful rendition. The remainder of the trip for that day was in absolute silence except for the sound of the hooves, the tinker of chain, and the crunch of wheels, crushing pebbles as they rolled. The twice daily checks of the dead and sick revealed its gruesome toll. On one occasion an infant was snatched from its mother's arms and thrown into the bush beside the road. The mother said not a word. It was later discovered that the child had been taken away at the request of the other slaves as it had been dead for many days.

One day, a horseman galloped in shouting that everyone should take cover. His horse dripped with sweat, its mouth frosted with saliva and the bridle was outlined in foam. Manta could see the heat rising from its body like a kettle of boiling water. "Take cover! Take cover, the Yankees are coming, the Yankees are coming!"

The noise aroused Nelly who whispered aloud, "Who Yankee?" There was no reply to her question. The teams bolted into action, throwing the cargo of people violently about. When under cover of what could have been willow trees, the drivers left the wagons to quiet their horses. The outriders, with their whips, quietly threatened the people with their lives if a sound was to be made.

Nelly's lungs seemed to attempt to betray her. Manta clasped his hand over her mouth as one cough would surely have meant their death.

Minutes later, the air filled with sounds of thunderous hooves and wagons. Though Manta could not see the source of the confusion, the dust it created could be seen wafting through the trees, raining its irritation down on the lowly company of God's children. When the noise stopped and the dust had cleared, the complexion of many a dark soul had changed several shades lighter. It was here that Manta heard for the first time in his life, Virginia. He had heard one of the drivers say that it was a long way to Virginia. It was several days before anyone was allowed to get out of the wagons.

The smell of human waste seemed to irritate the drivers, whose tempers seemed to shorten with every mile. Taking shelter near a lake, the drivers gathered water for themselves and then watered all the horses before the people were allowed leave of the wagons. Many of them could not straighten out their semi-paralysed legs for quite some time. Nelly was one of them. After being struck many times to the head, Nelly clinging desperately to her dignity as well as to her child, fell face first into the water. This helped to soothe her parched throat and revive her spirit. There was no change of clothing and, of course, no lye soap, but wading deep enough helped to wash away some of the odour that permeated the air. Nelly, in a moment of weakness, burst into the song, "Wade in the water just like John." A man went into the water in an attempt to silence her mouth. But to no avail, the entire chorus of slaves broke into the song, commemorating the love of Jesus when he said, "Be baptized as John was baptized in the Spirit."

The invigoration of the water was all too short. The straw in the wagons were removed and the wagons were swabbed down with buckets of water. In a half hour the journey continued. The wet clothing and the coolness of the night caused Nelly to shiver beyond control and a violent fever overtook her. By morning, when the drivers came with the ration of potatoes, Nelly could not be wakened. Much to Manta's relief, the driver did not notice or did not care if she ate or not.

It was curious how the slavers had changed their tactics. They were now travelling by night and resting by day. On one occasion, the mosquitoes were so thick, that Manta spent most of the day fanning them away from his mother's face and body. His eyes were swollen practically shut from the bites of thousands.

On one occasion, the night rain fell in torrents. Thunder and lightning lit up the sky, silhouetting the shadowy ghost-like images of the weeping willows. This prompted Manta to cling even closer to his mother. The loud claps of thunder grew ever more intense, the wind howled and drove the cold, icy chill even deeper into their meager garments. Nelly consoled Manta as best she could and shielded his face, in the protection of her bosom, from the blistering rain. Manta, challenged by the thought that his mother may not last long, started to doubt whether or not there was a God. Truly this was not freedom.

His tears, camouflaged by the droplets of rain which peppered his face, plus the added discomfort of leaves and other debris that accompanied the strong winds, stung him beyond tolerance. In the dead of night he screamed for mercy, but the wagons never stopped, other than to move fallen branches out of the path of the horses.

They take my chillun away Lord.
I wish I never was born.

CHAPTER 5

March of Death

After what seemed to be months, the procession abruptly ended. They had arrived on the outskirts of a town and one of the horsemen went on ahead. The drivers seemed to be happier, and soon the special water was issued among them. They danced and sang. They finished their celebration by pulling many of the younger women off the wagons, stripped them naked, poured water over them to bathe without soap, using only the straw, which shielded the special water in its crate, as facecloths.

After an hour of screaming and beatings to those who resisted, the men sufficed themselves of their lust. The final insult came as a warning that anyone who interfered would also suffer. Still naked, the women were made to stand in the wagons, to now entice the male slaves into lusting after their flesh. However, no man cast his eyes upon them and many hours later, the girls collapsed on the floors of the wagons. The women among them covered them as best they could with their own meager garments.

The next day it became evident that the wagons would no longer be used, and then Manta realized what the chain wagons were for. The last selection of those who were healthy was now in play. All slaves were made to stand. First the men, one after another, were scrutinized by prying their mouths open to examine their teeth and gums. The examination was performed by an old man with white hair who talked strangely.

After the selection of the strong was performed, those chosen were then shackled together with leg irons. This task took longer than the examination.

The women were examined by the same man, who used a prod pressed firmly under the nose to force open their mouths. The older women were separated immediately. Nelly, for some reason, passed the test, whatever the test was for. Nelly, Manta and Bertha Samuels were examined. As she was young, Bertha passed with ease.

All children were allowed to be free of chains. The women, though not chained by the ankles as the men were, were however, linked to the men with the dreaded nigger yokes. The nigger yoke was a wooden oxen yoke type apparatus, linked together from slave to slave by a short piece of chain. A wooden spike was placed in the front of the yoke, pressing in the throat. A similar wooden spike was fixed in the back aimed at the base of the skull. This apparatus was designed to prevent all of those on the march from falling behind. The lead man was chosen because of his fitness. He had no yoke. All others were linked to him. If anyone behind him could not keep up, the spike behind his head would pierce the base of the skull, thus forcing him or her to keep up the pace.

In all, there were sixty-five men and some forty women; twenty-one people were unacceptable and were left behind. Their fate was not known. Twenty-four had crossed over the river Jordan and were swept up in the arms of Jesus.

This time there were no wagons, just outriders and pack horses. Each rider had a whip and the march commenced with great haste, as time seemed to be of the essence for some reason.

There were no roads, only a narrow trail. The horses were nervous as they pressed on through the bush. Manta was anxious about Nelly and prayed that her strength would hold. The march continued at a vigourous pace. Nelly kept pace only for Manta's sake. The trail was so narrow in places that Manta had to drop back for periods of time in order to get by.

Swamp and jungle-like terrain soon took its toll and at the day's end, all lay down exhausted. The humid air soon laid claim to Nelly's infected lungs. It was not long before her temperature rose to extremes beyond all help. Her water ration was wasted as Nelly could not comprehend what it was. Manta spent the night trying to keep the spike of the nigger yoke away from his mother's throat, as in her illness she lay awkwardly in an unconscious state. A ration of sugar cane was dropped at the feet of all at daybreak. All were nudged to their feet. After a feeble attempt to wake Nelly, a signal was sent ahead. Within minutes, a man came with tools and hammered at the yoke around Nelly's neck until it fell off in two pieces.

Though not dead, Nelly was dragged into the thicket and left there. Manta's heart wept as he knelt over her frail body. Nelly opened her eyes for the last time that he could recall, and with as much breath as she could muster, spoke her last words to her son, "You have been chosen, you are the Moses, the people need you, you must lead them. Promise me you will hate no one if I die. I die for my Lord."

The dream of a physical promised land, though believed by all, was obtained by a precious few. This truth had become a reality to Nelly. She knew the promised land was not hers to see and in the silence of night the angel of death appeared and took her home. With all the reverence and strength that a child could muster, Manta covered his mother with leaves and made a vow with his Lord, that no matter what his lot in life, he would serve Him until the end. He then removed the shoes, lashed by a flimsy piece of leather around her neck and placed them as best he could, on her swollen feet. Manta still remembered how his mother valued her shoes, and how fortunate she felt to have them. He also thought of the reason why the slavers did not allow shoes, and he thought if only he had a pair of shoes he could run so fast, even the slave drivers horses would never catch him. Emotion overcame him, in anger he cried aloud, clenching his fists in defiance to the devil.

As he watched his mother's life leave her body, he tried to remember the good times. He searched his mind in haste, only to find none. Good times, perhaps, were yet to come.

Rising to his feet, he tossed the last armful of leaves over his mother's face and departed.

Unnoticed, he fled in the opposite direction. By this time the procession of bond servants had long since passed. It was not long before his pace weakened. Overpowered by the lack of energy, Manta collapsed and could go no further. He could hear his mother's words of courage through the pulsation of every heart beat. "You are the chosen one, the Moses." Manta then knew what he must do. In order to help his people, he too had to give up his chance to escape to freedom and rejoin the group of souls in bondage.

The effort to overtake them gave Manta time to contemplate things. As he retraced his voyage, he returned to the spot where his mother's body lay.

With a heavy heart he took one last look and continued his trek back into bondage. The night drew near, but Manta knew that if he slept, he would never rejoin his people.

He walked throughout the night, until finally, Manta could hear voices, and see the faint glow of an exhausted fire. Without being noticed, Manta rejoined the troop of ailing, footsore children of God.

It was not long before Manta saw how he could help relieve the agony of his people, and he started his labour of love by washing many a swollen, pebble-bruised foot. He saw to it that all were given water and made certain that what little rations there were available were shared by all. Those who stumbled, he helped to their feet. He also bandaged wounds. There were many people who needed medication, ointment for their feet, but there was none. But many a soul welcomed the mud poultice that Manta applied to their feet while they rested. He searched through filthy, dust-filled hair and removed ticks; thus giving thankful relief from certain torture, as the shackles and yokes prevented them from scratching their heads to remove the vermin that were present. He scratched their backs, removed splinters, and did whatever else he could to help relieve the misery of his people. Most of all he prayed for and with every man, woman, and child. Those who fell by the wayside, he lifted to their feet and he acted as a crutch for those who were weak.

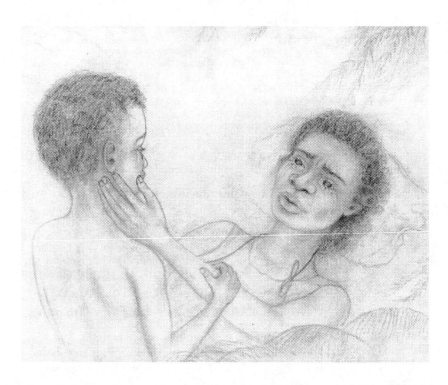

When fires were permitted during the march, Manta saw to it that the fires were fueled to keep his people warm throughout the night. When permitted, he kindled several fires so that the majority could benefit from the blessed warmth, which drew the cold of the nights away from the bodies of men, women and children who were susceptible to pneumonia, colds, and fever. He encouraged them to sing God's praises and reminded them that God promised that his people would one day be free. Before long Manta had earned the respect, or at least touched the heart, of the slavers and slaves alike. In the quiet times at night, the men encouraged Manta to sing to them. Soon the entire chorus of a hundred voices or more rang out in song - thus consoling them with the very songs of yearning which freed the minds and attitudes of enslaved people for generations.

Unknown to the slave drivers, these songs gave the people courage, hope, and a firmer grip on God's love. The kindness Manta shared seemed to be addictive. So much so, that the slavers many times allowed two rest periods a day rather than one, and allowed extra water rations. On one occasion when a child was taken home to glory, a slaver insisted that the body be buried and prayed over.

Satan's Voyage

After what to Manta, seemed to be months and months, the company of people lay exhausted in the shade and cover of the woods. A strange sound could be heard; even the slavers were mystified as to its origin. In some ways it sounded like a distant clap of thunder, but this thunder seemed to have a rhythm which clapped at the same intervals. Only one among the slavers had heard this sound before, and called the sound waves. Manta, curious as to what a wave was, walked toward the mysterious sound. He walked no longer than twenty minutes, when to his fascination, he saw a sight he had never seen or even imagined he would ever see. The noise, he found, was a huge body of water rolling toward the shoreline. Manta's mind was boggled at such a breathtaking sight. Dumbfounded, he watched the waves clap against the rocks below him. For several minutes he could not comprehend what all this water could mean. He wondered if perhaps this was the great flood that Noah experienced. If so, could it be possible that he would meet Noah? Backing away from the vast ocean, he raced back to the spot where the others lay to tell what he had seen. His explanation of the Great Flood brought about a roar of laughter from the man who called this thing a wave. He tried to describe the smell of salt as well. What was all this water about?

All too soon Manta and all the brethren would know what this vast body of water was all about. It was not too much longer in their journey, that all eyes were to behold the great wonderment of the Atlantic Ocean.

Never in Manta's wildest imagination could he have imagined the events which took place within the weeks that followed. The ocean could be seen at all times now to the right of them. The slavers seemed to be joyous that the trip would be over in a day or two, and finally the journey ended.

Immediately the slaves were placed in the hands of others who herded them into a barn built over the water. Manta could see the water through the gaps in the flooring of the building. The smell of fish, salt and body perspiration was a definite sign to Manta that his days of slavery were not over.

The new slavers were all strangers and spoke strangely. Manta could understand what they said only if he listened hard to what they had to say.

The next day, to the joy of all, the yokes were removed, which prompted the people to once again praise the Lord in song, "Goin' lay down dat burden, goin' leave it with the Lord."

In the silence of the night, all were herded aboard a ship. Once again a new chapter unveiled itself. Some hundred souls were crammed into the hole of a vessel which could not house fifty in comfort.

The strange surroundings drew fear in the hearts of all. There were no port holes to allow air or light. Still shackled, all lay in silence in the dark, so dark was it that not a glimmer of light invaded their entombment. Manta could feel only the movement of the ship, but knew not what was happening. The movement of the ship for some time, tossed people to and fro with negative results. Many, in particular the children, emptied the contents of their stomachs. Soon the smell of spew competed with any available air. Perspiration added its fume with all the other elements, causing a putrid smell so great that those who were ill, soon succumbed to disease.

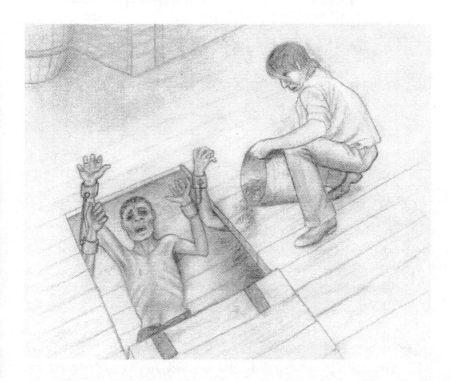

On the third day at sea a hatch door opened, shedding a blinding light into the hole. Though glorious, no one could appreciate its value over the cool breeze which wafted in with the light. At the same time, raw potatoes, carrots, and some other type of vegetable were thrown into the hole. Immediately thereafter, all light and air was snuffed. The search for food in the darkness began. Manta instructed that no one move, so in the darkness, food was passed around until all had been served.

The following day, the majority of people were sick. Thirst overcame them in such a way, that many men urinated in their hands and slurped the awful by-product into their mouths. The next day the hatch opened again. The stench was so strong that the slavers would not enter, but lowered an open-ended keg of water into the hole. Losing control of themselves, all tried to secure a sip of water. The darkness made it impossible to distribute the precious liquid and before long, all was capsized onto the floor, causing panic. Those who sat nearby wet their hands from the floor and lapping like dogs, tried to secure a drop of moisture on their lips.

It is not really known how long the journey lasted. It is surmised that it was about two and a half weeks.

The hatch opened for the last time, all who were alive were ordered to stand. Only the very young were able to, as most had not stood for the entire journey. Manta and a few others moved toward the hatch where there had been a ladder lowered. It took all the strength that Manta had to climb it. Reaching the portals, he had to shield his eyes from the blinding light. Focusing his eyes as best he could to see in the distance, there was land all around him. For the first time he saw the vessel that had housed him for so long. The vast body of the water was scary. They were on top of the Great Flood. He wondered if this was the great boat that Noah had built, however, there were no animals. Slowly the deck filled with souls in bondage. Manta shifted his way toward the hole, peering into the darkness, and stomaching the stench as best he could, he could see the bodies of many.

A company of men reluctantly entered the hole to remove the bodies. Ropes were lowered from above, attached, and were hauled to the surface with body after body.

Manta in his short life on earth had seen his share of death, but the ultimate anxiety seized his heart and mind when, while watching the removal, the body of Bertha was hauled up and cast in to the sea with some thirty or forty others. Manta could do nothing to help. Heartbroken, he cursed at the Lord under his breath, "How can there be a God, a God who promises us a promised land, a God who says children come unto me, then he let dis child die like dis." His anger soon was dispelled with the aid of a whip, as those who remained were herded to one side while a small boat was lowered into the water.

A long rope was attached to it and fastened to the ship. The next orders sent Manta into instant panic, as all were ordered over the side. Manta could not swim and shuffled himself behind the pack, hoping something would happen so that he would not have to join the others. Man after man slid over the edge, holding on to the only life line that was available. This exercise, it was believed, was an attempt to clean up the slaves. However, to Manta's horror, there were some who chose to end it all by letting go of the life line. About seven in all sank quickly to the bottom, they had surrendered to the call of Satan. Defying the odds, they were never seen again.

The anger of losing these men caused some of the crewmen on board to argue among themselves, as no doubt, their profit depended upon the amount of live bodies they delivered.

Manta, too, contemplated the idea, though he was not shackled, he thought of just letting go . . .

The water was indeed refreshing. The taste of salt in his mouth was like nothing he had ever tasted. His vow to his mother dispelled the idea of surrendering to Satan. Though he did not know the future, he was determined to explore it in the great attempt to help his people. When all were aboard and counted, they were ordered to sit on the deck and were guarded by men with guns. The ship again set sail and headed toward the islands. As the ship cut through the waves, the bodies of some who did not survive floated away in the swells as the ship gained momentum.

Under full sail, the ship moved quickly toward the shore. At dusk, the ship anchored in what appeared to be a bay. At this time all were fed. This meal was probably the best ever. This was the first time since their escapade began that a hot meal was served. This meal consisted of cooked fish, rice, and some type of fruit called a loquat, all they could eat. Manta ate until he could eat no more. Water was in abundance and was served in tin cups. Late that night everyone lay asleep on the deck. A smaller vessel pulled alongside and Manta could hear the frantic voices of men arguing.

Manta heard the man who was still standing in the boat say that the British had long since abolished slavery. "They want you to separate the children." the man said. At that, a cry of anguish rang out from a mother whose child was also on board. Before Manta could adjust his eyes to see who, a slaver hit her and continued his conversation "Men and women stay on board, the children we put over the side near that island."

"Who will pay us?" demanded another.

"Get rid of these people first, then you will be paid."

There's no hiding place down there,
There's no hiding place down there,
O, I went to the rocks to hide my face,
The Rocks cried out "No hiding place!"
There's no hiding place down there.

CHAPTER 6

Marooned!

The next day, bright and early, Manta and all of the remaining children were loaded in two boats and rowed to a nearby island. No provisions were given, nor were they given any advice on how to survive. Marooned!

As the sun rose higher into the sky, Manta could see the splendour of God's handiwork. For the first time in his life he noticed the colour of the sky. The tall, majestic palm trees towered above them, the beautiful colour of the water and the warm winds swept at their faces. However, the beauty of the scenery was soon overcome with the reality that now all of these children had to be fed and given water. Where do they sleep? What do they eat? Are there other people here? Are there wild animals? There were myriads of other things to think about too.

Manta, as he was the oldest, took charge. First, he assured the children who had just been separated from their parents that one day they would see them again. But the majority of the children had been orphaned long before. The first order of the day was to thank Jesus for safely bringing them here alive and ask for guidance as to what to do to survive. In all, there were twenty-two, none of which Manta knew by name. He soon gathered them together and led them away from the beach into the cover of a nearby hill.

The search for food commenced immediately after instructions to the children to remain where they were and to stay quiet. Manta headed into the unknown in search of food. Manta tasted many wild fruits, not knowing what was poisonous.

On his journey back, Manta sampled all and hid them among the brush. On his return, he told the children that he had found no food, but promised to continue the search after they had built shelters for themselves.

The flimsy architectural structure proved to be successful. By using the huge leaves of palm trees and building a cradle above them as a lean-to, the children were at least kept dry from the salt air. They were soon asleep. But Manta stayed awake all night in prayer, asking his Heavenly Father for guidance.

The following morning, having tested the fruit he had eaten the day before, Manta felt strong and well. Now he felt that he could give what he had found to the others, allowing them samples of fruit that was safe. Everyone ate until full. Manta again led the children in praise to a God that had truly led them out of hell.

After eating their fill, Manta led all the children along the shoreline on an exploration trip to see what was on the island.

He decided to explore his surroundings, to estimate the size of the island, to find who, if anybody, inhabited it and if there was water. The troop started out in silence. Manta, fearing danger if they were found, made silence the order.

Manta was astounded by the beauty of the landscape. Staying on the beach, the children started the long trek. Manta hoped that they would not get lost. Thoughts crowded his head. Were there wild animals? Was there water? Would the great flood get any higher? He prayed that it would not rain so that the great flood would not rise higher and drown them all, as it would be a shame if all these little chillun would be taken away. Manta grew fearful that God had entrusted him with a task too great for him to handle.

He tried to think of what Old Isaac would have done in this situation. The peacefulness of the surroundings was in a sense calming, however, the strangeness still drew a fear of the unknown.

Nothing was familiar to Manta. The trees, the grass, the air, even the very sky was a different colour. Manta looked out across the great flood, and could see in the far, far, distance another speck of land that appeared as though it had ascended from the deep. Straining his eyes, he tried to guess the distance in regards to its possible dangers. The children stayed close together and said not a word. The walk took about three hours before Manta realized that he recognized familiar surroundings. Soon they came to the very spot where they had started. Manta then realized that they had in fact walked the circumference of the island. During the entire walk Manta saw nothing that he felt could harm them and already was planning tomorrow's trek through the centre of this island of paradise. He felt if he could walk from end to end through the centre of the jungle-like shrubbery, this would certainly ease his mind as to the dangers that this place might produce. The children were told once again to be silent as they returned to their shelter.

Manta gathered as many palm leaves as he could, making as little noise as possible. He strengthened the shabby structure as best he could. The sun hung low and as the children slept, Manta could see beads of sweat appear on their foreheads.

Manta wondered if this meant sickness had befallen the children. Wiping his own brow he was somewhat consoled by the fact that he too had the same symptoms, but he felt fine. As the children slept, Manta took the opportunity to explore this island a little further. He decided to challenge the highest hill he saw, and when conquered, he discovered to his delight that he could see the entire island from this vantage point. From here, Manta scanned very carefully over the landscape in search of wild animals, he could hear nothing other than the chirping of the birds and the rolling swells breaking upon the shore. Manta consoled himself with the idea that the only thing he had to worry about was the great flood. Surely it could never get higher than this hill. This comforting enlightenment actually drew some happiness to his heart as Manta trod the long path down.

When Manta arrived back at the encampment, the children

were at play on the beach. Manta had to stop himself from chastising them for breaking the silence. For the first time in many years Manta, heard laughter. The children were fascinated with a strange shelled animal on the beach and were unaware of the dangers of teasing a land crab by prodding it with sticks. Before too long, the inevitable befell them. A youngster, no older than three, was the unfortunate victim of the angry crustacean, who decided to enforce his might in warfare by clamping a claw on a baby toe. The atmosphere changed from laughter to tears. Manta, springing to the aid of the child, snatched him from the beach, but the beast hung on and the cry of anguish grew even stronger. Manta grabbed the beast in an attempt to remove it and became its second victim. The discomfort of it all forced Manta to throw it to the ground, and he watched as it scurried under the sand. Manta hushed the children to silence and hurried them away from the sands. "If these things live under the sand, they could come up and bite your toes," was the explantation given. For many days thereafter the children would not walk on the sand. Manta did not mind this at all because it was successful in keeping the children away from the water.

Manta's worst fears seemed to be materializing when one morning he noticed, for the first time, that the waters of the great flood had risen and rose above the shoreline. Immediately he ordered the children to follow him up into the high hill. The climb was tedious, but all made it with a minimum of cuts and bruises.

The immediate search for shelter began. Palm leaves were gathered and soon makeshift shelters were constructed. The abundance of food, the apparent lack of danger, the awesome reality made Manta wonder if this was indeed the Promised Land, but what of the rising waters? Manta watched intently as the tide came in. To his astonishment, during his vigil, he also watched as the great flood waters subsided and the tide went out. Manta decided that the camp must remain on the hill for the safety of the children.

The day's activity started and ended with prayer. The God of Moses, Noah and John was consulted at every move. The songs of the Spirit were sung at every circumstance, be it good or bad.

It is believed that on or about the fifth week there rose a great storm. The rain came in torrents, the violent winds ripped the vegetation from the ground, the huge trees bowed toward the earth, yielding their fruit to the powers of the wind as the roar of the surf gnawed at the sand on the beach, revealing the hidden stones beneath.

The palm leaf shelter did not hold even for an instant, but was blown violently into the abyss leaving the children naked of precious shelter. Huddled together, they clung to whatever their little hands could grasp. The sky blackened the sun with clouds in a strange way that Manta had never witnessed before. Then lightning ripped from the clouds which lit up the sky as bright as day, thunder exploded above them with a great rumble. Fear and trepidation gripped the children as they lay face-down and the rain peppered their backs.

The storm abated as suddenly as it began, the absolute stillness drew Manta to his knees. He opened his eyes, and to his horror, he discovered that all of the beach was devastated. Manta could not believe the destruction. The silence was almost unbearable. The sea had lost its colour and was without a wave. The sky was blackish-grey all around. Manta's eyes focused on a beautiful blue spot in the water, this confused him beyond means. Suddenly one of the children cried, "Look, look!" Manta turned toward the excited cry to find that all had their eyes turned toward the heavens. He could not believe his eyes. Looking up he saw a perfect circle of blue in the sky, while all around it was a black swirling cloud. He soon found the source of the blue spot on the waters. Yes, they were caught in the eye of a storm.

So beautiful was the sight that Manta laid on his back with his hands behind his head to behold the wondrous beauty of such a spectacle. Truly this was the Promised Land, but how could something so treacherous be so beautiful? These thoughts brought to mind his vow to God and his own mother when he promised to hate no man. Could there actually be some good in the torture he and his mother had endured under the hands of their captors?

Manta knew that the inner man in him was right. Although he had prayed for guidance, healing,strength, hope, patience, trust, kindness, and many times mercy; he realized the he had never yet prayed for forgiveness for those who had enslaved him. Finally, he laid back and surrendered it all to God. He forgave all that had ever happened to him and everyone who had inflicted pain on him. It was here that Manta felt for the first time that he too had to be forgiven.

The black clouds that encircled the beautiful blue opening were picking up momentum. The faster the clouds circled the opening, the smaller it got. The winds once again roared, the rains continued, and lightening and thunder exploded above them once again. The children huddled closely together and said not a word. Manta tried to give words of comfort which could not be heard above the noises of the storm. The storm raged on for an hour and as suddenly as it came, it subsided.

The sun reappeared, the winds continued to dissipate until, finally, all was normal.

All but the food supply! The fruit trees were barren of fruit. Many trees no longer stood. The banana trees and their yield were blown away, there was nothing . . .

Manta's Search

Manta was concerned that the only moisture the children received came from the fruit which was their main source of nourishment. The sudden absence of it soon brought home a strange reality that though for weeks now the children had eaten well, they still for some reason grew thinner. Looking at himself, he noticed that he too had lost weight. Could it be that they had not even had a cup of water in weeks or were they all getting ill? Manta left the group and frantically searched for food. He returned hours later with but a handful of fruit which was pounded into mush, a non-appetizing mush. He wondered if the great flood would rise up and devour them through the night. The damp clothing of the children made them shiver. Manta longed for the comforts of a nice warm fire. Before long Manta had the children marching in a circle pretending that they were marching around the great walls of Jericho. Soon all were dry.

Manta knew that he must find water, food, proper shelter and a way to light a fire. As the children lay quiet in the night, Manta looked toward the speck of land that he had seen some time before and wondered if there lay the answer to some of his problems. "If only I could get there," he thought. "I can't swim." All night Manta laid awake, wondering how, with the surf breaking on the shore and the wonderment of the stars above his head.

He realized how simple a task it would be if he stopped doubting and started believing. Soon his heart and mind, prodded by an inner voice, changed the tempo from "I can't" to "We must, we must," now meaning Jesus and him. We must because the children have no food or water, even though the great flood was all around them. Somehow it was poisoned and the children were ordered not to drink it. Questions ran through his mind as to why they could not drink from the great flood. Perhaps because Noah had only his family on the great ship. There must be a lot of dead men and animals beneath the water. That's why the water tasted bad, he thought as he spat on the ground to clean his mouth, which once again reminded him that now they must find water.

Manta spent the night in prayer, seeking an answer

from a higher power. He arose the next morning full of new hope. Though he got no sleep, he was full of energy and somehow he knew that all would be well. Gathering the children together, he took them on a march throughout the island. He formed them into a straight line, even though at that time he was not sure why. He soon noticed that the huge leaves of banana trees that had collapsed on the ground, also held pockets of water. Kneeling to taste the water, Manta realized that the water rose up around his knees. Though the children were anxious to drink, Manta reminded them that this could also be the dead water from the great flood and may not be safe to drink. Clasping his hands together, he drank some of the water from the banana leaf. He found it to be fresh and clean. He then instructed the children to look for other big leaves and to drink the water from them.

Manta realized that had he not kept the children in a line, this valuable supply may have all been trampled and lost into the earth. It was not long before all the children found enough water to drink.

"But what about tomorrow?" Manta thought, fighting back the negative thoughts. Manta reminded himself of when he had heard Old Isaac say, "First we must live for today, tomorrow is promised to nobody." With this in mind, Manta led the children in prayer for the day's blessing.

The next day the children were led, once again in line, this time to encircle the island. On one shore they discovered that there seemed to be hundreds of brown, hairy, ball-shaped objects. Manta knew that they had fallen from the trees, as he had seen the same things on the great trees when he first came to the islands weeks ago. A decision was made to retrieve them from the great flood, though no one dared step into it. Finally Manta, holding back his fear, took his first step into the deep. His mind reflected back to the men who let go and sank beneath the waters and disappeared. He also remembered how refreshing it was and how clean he smelled after he had dunked into the great flood.

With this behind him, he removed all of the floating

fruit. The children, though hesitant because of the land crabs, walked on the sand and carried them all to shore. There were hundreds of them! Though Manta did not quite know why he was doing this, he made the children pack them all on the banks. Then the rest of the day was spent in transporting them up the high hill to camp.

The children lay exhausted when finally the laborious job was over. Manta consoled himself by thinking that even if these things were useless, at least it gave the children something to do, thus keeping their minds off of their hunger and thirst. Because these things were in the great flood, even Manta handled them with caution. That night he lay awake all night, trying to decipher a strange dream that he could not put out of his mind. The dream reminded him of the story of the children of Israel, who wanted to turn back, when according to Old Isaac, "De food fall right out of de sky, yes sir. Right out de sky."

It was early in the morning when Manta jumped to his feet, waking all of the children with him. "It be food! It be food!" Picking up the fruit, he shook it. It sounded like water. After several attempts at smashing it on the ground without success, he threw it against another. To his surprise, there leaked from it a white water. Holding it in has hands, he called the children in prayer, saying that if this is from the great flood, I may die. The prayer was short as the precious fluid was dripping away. Manta, closing his eyes, drank the water and to his surprise it was sweet and tasted wonderful, like nothing he had ever tasted before. Forbidding the children to drink likewise until all was safe, Manta also noticed that the inner shell was white and tasty. Plucking the white inner lining out of the shell as best he could, he ate it all. The next morning, Manta and the children had a feast on food which fell from heaven. Manta was even more thankful that he could see some of the fruit, which still remained, on the few trees that survived the storm.

Surely this must be the Promised Land! The children prayed and sang more songs of the Spirit. For some reason the children became less afraid of the great flood, and after awhile all began to wade in the water. Was this the cleansing waters that Isaac talked about? How did he know? These questions lived with Manta for many weeks.

Manta knew that the food falling from heaven supplied only two of their needs. He knew that his quest for the warmth of a fire was going to involve him travelling to the other island. How? He was still unsure . . .

One day, he looked around and saw before him twenty runny noses, and realized that he could hold out no longer. He informed the children that he was going to take a journey and pointed toward the island they could barely see. After some brief explanation as to why, he knelt in prayer, asking guidance if this was the right thing to do. The answer came to Manta during the night as he paced up and down the beach while the children slept. The quarter moon lit up the sky and silhouetted the white sand beach where Manta came upon a log which had drifted ashore. It was here that Manta found his answer to the transportation problem. He pulled the log ashore far enough so that the great flood would not rise and carry it away. Manta had noticed this happen many times before.

Wade in the water,
Wade in the water, children.
Wade in the water,
God's gonna trouble the water.

CHAPTER 7

The Journey

The next morning the children gathered together with Manta on the beach. Once again they prayed for a safe journey.

It was now that Manta realized that through it all he did not know the names of any of them. He wanted to select one among them to be leader while he was away.

The decision did not take long. Quickly, asking the Lord to help, he chose one of the older boys who was a good prayer. "This was more important than strength," thought Manta.

The children, after promising to obey and pray every day, helped Manta roll the log back into the sea. Here Manta removed his flimsy shirt and placed in it four coconuts, "the food from heaven," and balanced them on the log then straddled himself over it. Using his hands and arms as oars, he paddled himself out to sea, toward the faraway island. The children watched as he drifted out of sight.

Manta did not stop all that day. When the sun disappeared as it fell into the sea, the eerie darkness drew fear in his heart, so much that he stopped paddling to pray. During the prayer he fell asleep.

When he awoke, it was obviously morning. Manta was fearful because he could no longer see the island which was his goal and he cursed himself for falling asleep. He was not sure whether he drifted in circles or even if he was still facing the right direction. The waters were as calm as the wind after the storm. "If only I could stand," thought Manta, "What if I fall? I can't swim. But I must know which way I am going." With these thoughts behind him, he attempted to stand up, unsuccessfully. He fell into the water. His attempt to stand not only dumped him in the water, but he also lost the cache of food and even worse, his precious supply of water from the coconuts. Discouraged, he pulled himself up on the log again and asked God for guidance.

Weeping aloud, he questioned if this was the right thing to do. Shortly thereafter, he sat up on the log with his legs still straddled over it, and with his feet still in the water. He could feel the cool wind blow against his back. He realized that every time he had looked upon the island the wind was at his back; even the day he started the journey the wind was at his back.

It was not until the third day of his journey that he encountered three strange objects knifing their way toward him. What were they? Manta was soon to find out. The objects were shaped like the big cloths on the slaver's ship. As the shapes surrounded the log, Manta could clearly see that the objects were huge fish. He watched horrified for hours as the fish circled him. Finally they disappeared and Manta, though fearful to put his arms back into the water, continued to row toward the unknown. That night the winds arose from behind him and the calm sea soon turned treacherous. The waves were immense. Manta held on until his fingers were numb. Many times the log plunged beneath the sea, but Manta held on gasping for air every time he ascended. This continued throughout the night and for most of the next day. Manta found that the movement of the log seemed easier while the wind was behind him. His hunger and thirst grew heavy. He knew that he must either find food and water or die.

Very late the following night, Manta could hear the familiar sound of the surf pounding the shore. Manta's heart joyfully pounded in rhythm with the surf, as he knew that he must have reached the shore. Though the moon was now half, in the position he lay, he still could not clearly see that his journey would soon be over. As the last swell hit him, it drove him and the vessel hard against the shore.

Manta realized that he had hit something hard and

sharp. Letting go of the log, Manta clung to the rocky shoreline with sharp rocks cutting at his hands and feet. The waves were still slamming him and the log against the shore. With great strength, Manta managed to defeat the great suction of the waves to pull him back out to sea, and with hands and feet bleeding, he managed to climb ashore. Exhausted, he laid there until the sun woke him.

Looking around, he found that this island was way bigger than the island he had left. There was no sand, it was hard rock and very sharp. His hands and feet were still stinging with pain. He pulled his way to the summit of the hill to look around. He saw no signs of life but many trees looked familiar. The "isle of paradise" he had just left had the same trees. This was a great comfort to Manta as he now knew there was plenty of food. He soon learned that the great storm had hit this island too, as many of its trees were in ruin. Eating as much as he could salvage and quenching his thirst with as many "fruit from heaven" as he could find, he set out to explore the unknown. Following the shoreline, he soon made his first startling discovery. Voices appeared to come from the sea.

Peering very cautiously over the cliff edge, so as not to disturb anyone, Manta could see two men in a small boat who were pulling something into it. Though these men were brown, Manta determined that they were not slaves. He had heard the strange language before, especially on the slave ship. Manta soon understood that they were fishing. He watched with great interest as the men cast their nets into the sea again and again.

Manta had never seen fishing like this. He had watched Old Isaac fish many times before with an old pole and a long thin piece of leather with a big knot on the end and pieces of corn stuck in the knot. He remembered as if it were yesterday. Isaac noisily shouting for joy when he caught the big one! How he boasted that to be a great fisherman like him, you had to grow up strong and quick and your eyes had to be jus' right to catch de big ones. Manta soon forgot the pleasant memory when he caught the eye of one of the men who appeared to have spotted him. Under cover of the dense trees, Manta slipped away. Gathering several large rocks to be stacked upon each other, he marked the spot where he landed. He stopped only to thank his Lord for delivering him safely thus far and continued his journey inland.

It was two, maybe three hours later, that Manta came upon a road. He could see that it was used, as he could see the tracks of wagons and hooves were imprinted in it. Manta soon surmised that if he followed the road it had to lead to something or somewhere. He travelled the road by night and slept by day. Two nights later, aided by the moon, he came upon an old barn right beside the road. It appeared to be abandoned. Manta laid in the soft hay to rest and fell asleep.

Manta was jolted to his knees at the sound of a loud noise and a sudden bright burst of sunlight which blinded his eyes for a moment. While adjusting his eyes, to his horror, in the haze of dew, dust and sunlight there stood before him an old man. Manta sprang to his feet. "You be one of them niggers everybody's talking about? Well, you don't belong here."

Manta, backing away, found himself trapped in the back of the barn, knowing that his only way out was past the angry intruder. "If I catch you boy, I'll have you whipped and send you back where you belong."

Manta bolted toward him in an attempt to get around him. He did not move, but hit Manta beside the face with a chain attached to a harness. Manta continued past him, his head split open and his eyes filled with blood from his lacerations. He ran into the bush like a wounded dog. There he collapsed in pain.

When he awoke it was still daylight. Manta got the eerie feeling that something was definitely wrong. He ached all over. The dried blood on his face did not offer a clue as to what had happened to him. What was worse, was that he found himself climbing out of a shallow hole, covered mostly with leaves. Manta remembered nothing about how he got there. Pulling himself to his feet, Manta made the most horrifying discovery of all! Foot prints, several of them, made by people with shoes. This final discovery struck even greater fear in his heart. There before him, embedded in shallow top soil, was a spade. Manta then caught the full scope of his demise. He must have passed out, was found, beaten, and left for dead in this shallow grave!

Without any delay, he ran deeper into the brush until he came upon another barn and a cottage. From the shelter of the trees he watched until darkness closed in.

He then entered the barn to seek out what treasure he could find. He found some very familiar things which reminded him of his days of slavery. Potatoes were one, there were things which to Manta seemed to be onions and there were many ears of corn. Manta's mind grew wild with excitement. Why this is enough to feed all the children! He frantically stuffed every sack bag he could. In the middle of this procedure, Manta's inner voice argued with him about the validity of taking it all, and explained that he could, in fact, take what the children needed without taking several sacks, which would be impossible for him to carry. So he placed a dozen ears of corn, about a dozen or so potatoes, and several of the onion-like vegetables into the sack along with a long piece of hemp rope.

Manta set out toward the place where he thought he had landed. He felt led to return to the spot where he had been left for dead. It was almost sunrise when Manta reached the spot. Gazing into the shallow grave Manta was reminded of his mother. With tears in his eyes, he pulled the spade from the ground, used it as a staff and continued his journey. It then dawned on him that he was led there to get this tool. Manta, backtracking as best he could, travelled in the silence of night as the light of the moon was no more. But Manta, with his burden, continued. Before long Manta could hear the pounding of the surf against the shore.

Excited, he ran toward the sound. In the clearing, to his amazement, he had discovered a sandy beach. The fruit was in abundance. He sat to eat, to look out over the shore, and to pray. The darkness obscured his vision but in the haze, he could faintly see the waves break on the shore. Manta was confused because the landing point, for as far as the eye could see, had no sandy beaches. He again prayed for guidance and fell asleep.

That morning Manta was awakened by two familiar sounds. One was the surf and the second was the sound of the crowing of a rooster. Manta recalled eating a chicken egg cooked by Old Isaac on the long journey to freedom. He remembered that Isaac found the eggs in a nest near an old, abandoned farmyard. Old Isaac, however, could not catch the chicken. Manta, again arousing a good memory, proceeded to investigate the source of the noise.

Manta did not have to seek too long, as out of the trees strutted the rooster, and not too far behind him came the hen. Manta scanned the scene to see where the birds lived. He found that the team of feathered beasts were indeed quite a long way from home, as the nearest house seemed to be at least many, many running steps away. Manta baited the birds with a piece of ripe banana peel. To his delight the birds came closer than expected. When this trap was set, Manta lunged at the birds, grabbing the hen only, as the rooster did some strange dance on Manta's shoulder and fled to freedom.

The noise alerted a dog, which Manta could soon see was in pursuit of him. Manta, holding on to the hen by her legs, grabbed the other articles in his cache and ran as fast as he could. When he hit the road, his sore feet dug in and swiftly carried him away. Within minutes, the hound's bark was a long distance behind him. Manta had not even stopped to think about the point of landing. He ran as long as he could. When he stopped to rest, he could once again hear the swells slam against the shore.

Manta knew he was close, as the sound of the surf was like the thunder that he was familiar with, nor would he ever forget the sound of the great flood as it slammed him up against the rocks. The dog had chased him in the right direction. Had he entered the water on the other side he surely would have been lost, as that was the south side of the island. Manta needed to enter on the north, as his paradise isle was some eight miles at sea on the north shore.

Manta looked for his marker for many hours. Finally just before dusk, he found it. He knelt again to thank his Lord for delivering him back to the spot. Tying a piece of hemp around one leg of the chicken, he held it so that it could wander to eat, yet it could be retrieved.

The next morning Manta peered over the cliff once again, and to his surprise, his craft had washed ashore and was wedged among the sharp rocks. Manta surveyed the horizon to see if he could spot his island of paradise, but he could see nothing. He deduced that his island was too small to see as he had a hard time seeing this island which was much bigger. After consulting his Lord once again, he hung the chicken over his back, and amid a furious flapping of chicken wings, he set out to climb down the sharp rock to retrieve the log. After many painful minutes, he finally claimed his prize. Lashing the sack and the spade firmly to the log and securing the hemp to the log so that it would not drift away, he threw the log into the sea. He then removed the unhappy chicken from his back and lashed her in place. He straddled the log as before and again paddled away toward freedom.

Manta's only navigational tool was that the wind would now be at his chest. However, he firmly believed that his prayers before he set himself adrift gave him the finest navigator there was, as he was sure that the Holy Spirit would guide him home.

It seemed like hours later when Manta looked back. To his great discouragement he could still see the big island. He knew this time he must paddle through the night or he might just be swept backward. His arms grew too tired to continue. Manta knew that the current could very easily overcome him if he stopped rowing. In desperation, Manta unlashed the spade, sat up on the log with his feet still dangling in the water, and using the spade as an oar, he rowed onward. After awhile he managed to get the log moving forward in a straight line. The hen was quite unimpressed at being tied to the log, but seemed to be very afraid of the water. Manta fed her a piece of banana, but she would not eat. By the day's end Manta, looking back, finally felt satisfied that he was advancing. However, he still could not see his little island.

The darkness came all to soon bringing with it even greater problems. Manta could see that the great fish he had previously encountered were circling him again as he sat huddled on the log. There were now four of them as he sat in fear. He could see their huge bodies beneath the water. They were about three times the length of the log. They circled the log, even in the dark. Manta lay down on the log, drew up his legs and prayed that God would deliver him from the great fish. Suddenly it started to rain. The water came in torrents and peppered his body beyond belief. The hen cowered under her feathers and did not move. The rain subsided within the hour, but to Manta's amazement, the big fish were not to be seen. Exhausted, he lay flat on the log and fell asleep.

At daylight Manta looked behind to see if the big island was still out of sight. He could see nothing, but what he did see drew fear in his heart. Far behind him he could see the sails of a large ship coming toward him. Manta could only envision that this ship was a slave ship. This made him row even harder. The frantic race to outrun the ship was in vain, as the ship headed straight for him. Manta, not knowing if he had been seen, slid over the side and held on. The great ship, still charging down on him, passed within inches and continued its journey. Manta wondered where they were heading. He hoped that they would not see the children on the island. The sails grew smaller until finally it disappeared out of sight.

Manta's problems, however, had just begun. In anxiousness to watch the movements of the ship, Manta had little time to look around him. Suddenly a violent jolt struck him. When Manta could adjust his eyes to see the apparition that hit him he saw, to his horror, that he had been hit by the devil fish. Quickly, he sprawled up on the log once again. The devil fish attacked again and one gnawed at the log just ahead of where the hen sat. Amid the fluttering of wings and the spray of feathers, Manta watched the great, gasping mouth of the intruder, which left samples of its teeth in the log with every bite. Fear overcame Manta as he collapsed face down on the log, arms and feet sprawled into the water as the log drifted along the waves.

When Manta awoke, it was dark and silent. Searching about, Manta could feel the sharp edges of several teeth which were embedded in his craft. Attempting to sit upright, he fell backward into the sea. It was then that he discovered that his craft had been reduced by half. As he fell, the portion which remained up-ended, due to the weight of the sack and hen, submerged the hen under the water. Manta quickly righted the craft and hen and at once paddled onward. He hoped that the devil fish were asleep at night. The spade, though the handle was somewhat shorter, worked even better. Throughout the night Manta quivered with every sound, the most horrifying being that of a baby's cry which taunted Manta so much that he could take it no longer. He cried out in the dead of the night for help, somehow he knew he was not home. The cry of the child was mournful and sounded sinister. Was this the call of the dead? Manta tightly closed his eyes and with all the determination that he could muster, he rowed onward into the unknown. The mournful cry followed him throughout the night.

Just as light was to break the horizon, a great gush of water broke the surface shooting high into the air. Manta's eyes bulged with fear, straining to see what danger had befallen him. He could not see anything other than the water springing high into the sky and the huge dark shadow of a great beast. Submerged under him, Manta could not identify the object below him which surfaced only long enough to blow the tremendous spout of water high into the air. Manta realized that when the beast blew water, his feet sometimes touched the black object. He also noticed how the object grew even blacker as it surfaced.

Manta felt obsessed with rowing and before long, he could spot the island in the distance. As the day grew lighter, Manta grew more fearful because he could see the black shadow even more clearly. Even more shocking was the awesome sight as the beast raised its head out of the water to blow. Manta could see, for the first time, where the great source of water had come from. His vision clouded in the dark, Manta prayed that the beast would not turn toward him. But the beast seemed to travel at the speed that Manta could paddle. Never once did it pass completely under him, and Manta dared not overtake it for the fear that the beast would eat him.

Before long Manta could see the beautiful glitter from the pure white sand of the island's beaches, and almost as if it were planned, the great shadow descended into the depths of the Great Flood and disappeared. With a last show of strength, Manta paddled to exhaustion until he disembarked his vessel in waist-high water at the beach. Releasing the hen and dragging his cargo up on the beach, Manta collapsed into a deep sleep. He was home to his isle of paradise at last.

CHAPTER 8

Visitors

A few hours later, Manta was awakened by one small child, too scared to touch him, as they feared him to be dead, then when his lungs exhaled a groan, it sent the entire group scurrying in the opposite direction. However, soon the family was reunited and when the greetings were done, the gifts were shown and Manta told the story of his adventures and acted out each scene before the children. A prayer of thanksgiving ended the session, which lasted late into the night. Manta was among his children once again by the mercy of the Holy Spirit.

The next day, the job of planting potatoes began. Not knowing too much about gardening, the children dug a hole for each potato and they were scattered far and wide over the island.

The bright yellow onions were planted likewise. After some strict orders about how not to treat a chicken, the children refrained from running it down. That evening the children told their stories. Some needed to settle scores as to their treatment while Manta was away. Manta, after listening to all of their hardships, thanked God that all was well among them.

As the days went by, Manta and the children nurtured the plants and the tropical rains fell in abundance. Soon the fruit trees which remained began to heal and strengthen. Before long the island returned to paradise, as nature in all its fullness took over.

Manta realized that the only item on his list that he could not secure was fire. With the hemp he had brought home, he tried his hand at fishing as he had watched Old Isaac fish. It was easy! So tying a knot, into which was placed a piece of wood about six inches before the end of the hemp, he then used the remaining six inches to secure the bait which was a small fruit, bright yellow in colour (loquat). He then affixed a heavy stone about another three feet up the hemp. Manta then stood on the shore where the water was deepest and gently lowered the lure into the sea. When the heavy stone reached bottom, the wood filled knot floated, lifting the bright yellow berry until it was suspended three feet or so off the bottom. Staking his end firmly into the ground, the great trap was set.

Manta waited for hours staring deep into the depths to catch the elusive prize. For the first time Manta noticed the beautiful colours and variety of fish that there were in the great flood.

For many days Manta set his lines until eventually he had several set. As luck would have it, one day while checking the line, there before his eyes lay a big fish who had taken the bait and was overcome by the mastery of technology. Yes, this was the first yellow grunt of many, but how do you cook it with no fire?

The daily ritual of fishing soon proved to be successful. However, the attempts to dry the fish and the attempts to force the children to eat, needed yet a higher technology. So Manta decided to put off fishing until he had a fire to cook them.

Manta removed the sharp teeth from the log craft and found that the teeth of the devil fish, if used carefully, could be used as a knife to cut things. The dull ones soon became necklaces and trinkets.

As the days turned into weeks and weeks into months, Manta and the children prayed daily and thanked God for their freedom. With the help of the hemp and the use of the spade, the shelters were reinforced and even had palm tree windows which could be pulled up. Perched on the highest hill, Manta daily watched for hours for any sign of intruders.

The hot sun baked the sand on the beaches so that it was at times too hot to walk upon. This became a blessing to all, as one scalding day the hot sand prevented the children from playing on the beach. The children were amusing themselves in the shelter of the thicket when Manta noticed a large vessel, very much like the one that had brought them to this land. The sight of this spectacle weakened Manta with fear. As the vessel had dropped its anchor, Manta could see two small boats being lowered into the water.

Manta scurried through the thicket to warn the children. The children he did find were told to return to the campsite. There were only nine that he could find, the remaining children were at play in other parts of the island. Manta knew he had no time to warn them all and proceeded back up the hill to the campsite to see how far the boats had advanced upon them. To his surprise they were dangerously close. Manta, hushing the children to silence, peered out through the bush and watched the men disembark on the shore. He could clearly hear them say that they had returned to the island to find the children that they had dropped off many months ago. Yes, these were the same slavers and the very same ship!

Manta motioned the nine children into prayer. Fear gripped his heart for the others who were not in the safety of the palm leaf sanctuary. Manta hoped that the laughter and loud noises of the men would warn the others that danger was near. The men searched the island's beaches for signs of life but found none. Thankfully, the tide had been high the night before.

Manta feared that they would soon start to search inland. However, there was an argument among the visitors. One of the men insisted that there was no way that they could have survived. "They're dead, they're just children," he said. This seemed to convince most of the men to abandon the search. However, one man insisted that they keep looking as ordered. The others mockingly sat on the beach and advised him that all he would find was bones. The man started out into the bush.

Manta could clearly see him as he came directly

toward him. He again hushed the children into silence, took shelter in the trees, and prayed that the others had heard and had also taken shelter. All was silent other than the sound of brush breaking and the footsteps of the man approaching them. Manta and the children could see the man's feet. His worn boots were old and almost beyond repair. So close was he to them that Manta could have touched him. The feet turned in all directions, when suddenly a loud voice called out, "They're already dead, I tell you."

This froze Manta's heart beyond all efforts to remain calm.

"Come on, come on," the voice yelled. "Let's go!"

"O right, o right," the man yelled back.

Manta could see the boots turn and retrace their steps past them until they went out of sight into the thicket. The voices grew silent as Manta and the children watched the men board their vessels and row away. Soon afterwards, the remaining children rejoined the group. The spontaneous praise burst forth in song. Manta, in tears, thanked God for sparing their lives, as he knew that the men not only came to check up on them, but also to destroy all of those who remained. Manta directed the children to remain hidden until the great ship had set sail and was no longer to be seen on the Great Flood. The ship remained anchored until high tide and then set sail.

Naming God's Children

The children, for the first time, were asked to put names to themselves. First, the boy who was left in charge was named Luke. Though not strong in stature, he believed in prayer and seemed not afraid to rebuke Satan. He believed that they would all see the Promised Land. The smallest child, being only four years, did not know his name and seemed to be at times possessed by the devil. Sometimes his eyes would roll back into his head and he would wallow on the ground and make strange noises like a sick animal. Manta felt that God's children should have a name, so after an array of names the group agreed to the name Joseph. One by one the children came forth with a name. Rebecca, Joshua, two John's, Martha, Matthew, Lincoln, Thomas, Andrew, James, Eli, Sampson and Molly. Manta practiced these names daily while he was preparing to take yet another journey.

This time a much larger shopping list was prepared. These names he could practice during the lonely hours of the trip. Fire was top priority. Blankets, tools, vegetable seeds, something to boil fish and vegetables in , and if he could, he would steal a copy of the Great Book. Many days of preparation provided quite an elaborate craft with many innovative features. This was a two-logger, finely lashed together with hemp, and a hollowed out stump, strategically placed in the centre, held a good supply of small freshly dug potatoes, loquats, coconuts and a good sturdy stick to fight off the devil fish, and last but not least, two strong pieces of dry palm leaves which were excellent as paddles.

Second Journey

After much prayer, the vessel was set adrift upon the Great Flood once again. Manta, feeling much more secure as he did not have to lie down, knelt with great courage and rowed away once again into the unknown.

The engineering and craftsmanship, coupled with a great sea-worthy design, performed excellently for several hours until Manta noticed that hemp weakens when wet. Soon after the two logs were once again one. Looking back, Manta could no longer see his island, so once again he straddled upon one log with no food or water. Manta proceeded to paddle toward the big island for the second time.

He soon noticed that he had company, which jolted him once again to the reality of how vulnerable a child of

God can be on the Great Flood. Manta could see two dark objects surfacing beside him. His eyes were too tired from the constant strain to identify these objects. As the first object broke the surface, Manta knew that he had seen one of these before. It was a huge turtle, he and Isaac had caught one to eat. Manta instantly withdrew his hands and feet from the water as Isaac had said that a snapper could give you a mean bite. But the size of these could bite your whole arm off! The turtle appeared to solve its curiosity by criss-crossing the log and circling. Manta's eyes did not leave them for an instant until finally they both had disappeared beneath the surface of the sea.

The big island was still several miles away when daylight faded from the sky. The still black waters were deathly silent. Manta could hear only the noise of his paddle as it stroked through the water.

Manta pictured each child in his mind and practiced naming them all. This diversion from fear that raced through his heart was soon to be disrupted, as Manta could feel the presence of intruders; his heart pounded so strongly that he could hear it beat through his chest. In absolute silence, with his oar raised from the water, he could hear movement circling him from below. He could see absolutely nothing. Raising his legs as silently as he could from the waters, he lay face down on the log and prayed to his Lord that whatever was stalking him would go away.

Manta lay awake the entire night without movement. As the sun broke through the morning fog, Manta regained his visibility enough to see first hand his assailants. Two small devil fish, still circling him. Fear riveted his eyes on their fins that jutted through the water with the greatest ease.

As the fog lifted completely, Manta could see that he had drifted further down from the big island and realized that he had to start paddling or he could drift entirely past the island.

His attempts to frighten his predators, to Manta's horror, attracted two others to join in the game of torture. All

Manta could do was pray. He climbed to his knees and with eyes closed, he paddled nonstop until many hours later, when exhausted, he opened his eyes to find that he was once again alone.

But soon after, the very thing that Manta dreaded most happened. His paddle became water logged and broke under the strain. Manta had to once again use his hands and arms to paddle the craft.

Manta spent yet another night and a day before he came ashore on a sandy beach just before sunset. He was hungry, exhausted, but thankful that he had been spared once again. With one final burst of energy, he hid behind the huge cove of rock that sheltered the beach and fell asleep, his body limp. Awakening early, Manta realized the need for immediate planning. First he would find a safe place to hide. He would raid by night, hide by day, His search for a sanctuary did not take long. After an hour of climbing along sharp, rocky slopes, Manta discovered a cave embedded in a cliff wall. "No one will ever find me here.", he said to himself.

Manta cautiously climbed into its mouth. It was not large, but the wind had worn the rocks inside smooth and the roof was secure. The elevation was such that Manta could see for miles. Though Manta was well rested, he decided not to risk being caught in daylight. As thirsty and hungry as he was, he spent the day in prayer for his every wish and need. When bored, he recited the children's names and prayed for each of them.

Finally the day ended. The colour of his skin camouflaged him in the darkness as he climbed the cliff's edge. When he reached the top, he quickly marked the spot with stones and immediately set out to find life.

Under the cover of darkness, Manta's eyes and ears ached for the slightest sign of light or sound. His feet and legs were scratched beyond healing. The search continued. Many hours into the march, Manta's senses were tested to their fullest when he came upon a group of men seated around a fire. Apparently they were fishermen that had come ashore to eat and rest. Unnoticed, Manta stayed long enough to be captivated by the smell of fish and potatoes being cooked on the fire. The men said very little to each other. One man looked very much like someone Manta had seen as a child. Mama had called him an Indian. They were drinking special water too and this could only mean trouble, as the special water the slavers drank made them strange and angry. But Manta did notice that after the slavers got mad, argued, sometimes fought, they also fell asleep. Manta decided to stay hidden until the fire died and all three were asleep.

Manta surveyed the camp area for the treasures he needed, there were many possibilities. There was a lantern, two wooden barrels, some wooden spoons, even some blankets and knives. Manta wrestled with his inner man and worked up his nerve. Should he or shouldn't he move in now? His inner man won and persuaded Manta to circle the camp first. So in silence he made a wide circle around them and soon found himself standing on a cliff. Below him he could hear the waves smash against the shore in a rhythmic pattern that he was so familiar with. In the haze he could see set out before him hundreds of fish drying on wooden poles. He also discovered that the kegs contained salt.

Manta listened once again to his inner man who led him softly away and persuaded him to believe that these men would go fishing again tomorrow. While they fished it would be easier to obtain what was needed. Manta then positioned himself so that he could safely keep vigil over the men through the night. The sun rose and at the same time so did the men. Soon the smell of coffee filled the air. Manta's sense of taste went wild when Manta watched a man slowly open a sack. Manta's eyes bulged to see what tasty morsels were to be breakfast. Excitedly he watched as the old man's hand emerged slowly from the mouth of the sack. The treasure uncovered were eggs, but the most fascinating of all was a little shiny box from which the old man took two objects and laid them beside the ashes, he then removed the cap of a little jug and carefully poured some of the contents over the kindling. Manta's mind went back to his days with his mother, Isaac, the wolves, and the fire that saved their lives.

The man hit the two objects together close to the sticks and they ignited. Manta's heart jumped with joy, so much so that he almost gave himself away as something he did drew the attention of the men. For a moment all three looked in his direction, but soon dismissed the noise and continued their conversation. Manta learned that they fished until the hottest heat of the day and then they returned to clean, salt, and dry their catch. The smell of breakfast was a long torture to Manta as hunger and thirst had overcome him many, many days ago. Within minutes, the breakfast was over. The men set out toward the beach where two small boats were pulled up on the shore. Soon, the rhythm of oars propelled the boats out to sea.

Manta, famished, lunged at the sacks grabbing at anything edible. When the inner man abruptly interrupted, Manta stopped to listen once again and was made to realize that his prize was great, but he must not be greedy. Because of the distance away from his hide out, it would take several trips and might take several days to capture his precious supplies.

Manta grabbed at the two fire stones and the little metal container. He then realized that though this was his first priority, he must resist the temptation, the fire stones must be taken last. Whatever he took must not attract the attention of the men. They must not know that there were things missing. But how? Soon Manta had worked it out with help from the inner man. First he would take some of what there was most of, dried fish. So filling one of the many small, empty, wooden barrels with dried fish and gulping several mouthfuls of water from the water barrel, Manta immediately set out for the hide out. The long journey back wore him to exhaustion.

At around mid-day he had arrived safely. Hiding his stash carefully in the cave, he then decided to obtain some much needed nourishment by boldly biting into a morsel of raw dried fish. Manta's stomach, mind, and sense of taste could not agree. The stomach lost the battle forcing Manta to spit the horrible tasting food from his mouth. The heat of the day soon drained him of all energy and laid him out for several hours. He awoke to the sound of rain pounding the rocks around him. Leaving he cave he stood at its mouth, arms open wide toward heaven. He allowed the rain to drench him until his meager garments were soaked. His body refreshed and spirit renewed, he asked God's continued guidance and immediately started back toward the fishermen's camp, eating as much as he could find along the way. When he arrived at the camp he found the men busy at work. Surveying the site Manta noted that nothing was moved. The conversation of the men did not indicate that anything was wrong. Manta slipped further away to avoid being noticed.

The night once again revealed its blackness. The rain fell lightly, causing the night air to cool, as Manta shivered in his huddled position. He again rehearsed the names of the children and asked God to watch over them until he returned.

The next day his burden was much lighter. For this day he obtained three of many eggs, one of several spoons, a knife, one of many loaves of bread, and several handfuls of salt from a barrel. He placed them all in a sack and headed back to the cave. This time the journey was easier as the load was lighter. He again rested.

Manta awoke fresh and full of confidence. The sun was nearly asleep, so Manta hurried toward his goal. When he arrived, to his dismay, the fish had all been removed. Manta worried that the men had noticed the loss and suspected that something was wrong. Or was this their last day? He could also see that the wooden kegs were now stacked neatly on the beach. Manta grieved over the thought that he still did not have the fire stones and nervously contemplated their retrieval from the men. His prayer for bravery, plus desperation, drove him onward.

So in the early hours, when all lay asleep, the skulking figure of a boy crept among them and removed the fire stones, the kerosene, and one blanket which was at the feet of the big Indian man. Manta headed clumsily into the dark thinking all was well behind him. To his horror a tall dark figure stepped out in front of him. Manta's first instinct was to run, but he knew he should not run backward as he would truly be captured. Fear ripped at his heart and he fell unconscious to the ground. When he awoke he discovered that he was propped against a tree and kneeling directly in front of him was the big Indian.

Manta was in motion to speak when the Indian's big hand clasped his mouth and motioned Manta to silence. "You a slave?" the sibilant husky voice inquired.

Manta's mouth was still silenced by a big hand. The Indian placed his forefinger upon his lips to warn that he must speak quietly. Manta explained as quickly as he could but did not reveal his hiding place, nor did he mention the children or the island. Rising, the man pulled Manta to his feet, picked up the articles, placed them back into Manta's hands, and without a word turned and walked away. Manta did not hesitate. Clutching the fire rocks and bundle, he bolted into the darkness. Manta stumbled and fell several times but never stopped before reaching the mouth of the cave. His chest pounded in agony and his lungs ached. The sanctuary of the cave brought about a sense of peace and safety. He fell asleep clutching the fire stones, his most precious possession.

CHAPTER 9

Manta's Return

The next morning brought on its own set of problems as Manta realized he needed a bigger, safer vessel if he was going to get back with all his treasures. He had no hemp to lash logs together. In fact, he could find no logs to make a raft.

Manta racked his mind searching for answers to his dilemma. From his lookout he scanned the coastline, hoping to spot anything that would float. He could see nothing. He did not know how far down the coast he had drifted from the original landing place of his first voyage. He scanned the horizon in search of his little island but could find nothing. The answer, he thought, would be to walk the shoreline until he found the original place that he landed on his first voyage.

After praying to his Lord, he left the safety and cover of the cave in hopes of finding the vehicle to get him home and to find his bearings. Manta, using the cover of the rocks, worked his way unnoticed over many miles of beach and shore.

Much to his surprise, while he was working his way around a sandy knoll, he encountered a little village nestled among the hilly beaches in a beautiful bay, surrounded by trees that he had never seen before. Their leaves were the size of Manta's head and the bright red fruit was as sweet as sugar cane. Yes, Manta had stumbled upon a fishing village. This could be the answer to the problem. "If I could just find a small boat." he thought. Boats were in abundance and so were people.

Manta decided to wait until nightfall to get closer to the village. The many buildings, which were lit up, cast their reflections upon the still waters. Manta, all fear of the ocean behind him, silently climbed into the water holding on to whatever would keep him afloat. He pulled himself alongside the jetties which fronted the entire face of the village. Manta could hear music, the sound of people talking, and laughter. He could also hear the footsteps above his head. When Manta thought it was safe, he climbed up out of the water and laid on a ledge of soil and gravel which held up the footings for the jetties.

This made him even closer to his potential enemies, so close that had he wanted, he could touch their shoes by extending a finger through the slats of the jetty. As the night grew darker, the lower the temperature fell. The tide was getting higher, thus trapping Manta on the ledge. He watched the shadows give way to darkness and soon he gave way to the pull of nature himself and fell asleep.

Several hours later he awoke in horror when he discovered that he had been invaded by an army of land crabs. Though he was not bitten, the fear of having hundreds of the little beasts all over him drove him to panic, forcing him to roll off the ledge and into the water. The splash drew the attention of someone standing above, who called others to investigate. Manta, still in shock, held onto the sharp rocks in silence as he listened to the conversation above. After several minutes of suggestions, the crew above resorted to the fact that it was probably a shark and returned to whatever they had been doing. Manta's fears increased when he realized that the water was black with darkness and he could not see the bottom. He thought of the devil fish which might get him if he did not get out of the water.

When he felt safe to do so, Manta climbed up on the jetty. He searched for a vessel that would take him back to the island. The search did not take long. There before him lay a row boat, beached.

Without hesitation the boat was launched and the journey began, but not without problems. Manta soon discovered that his efforts to row away were hampered by a ship that turned only in circles! After many frantic moments, Manta did find the secret to rowing and managed to manoeuvre the craft away into the dark abyss. Though the blackness of the night obscured his vision, Manta knew that he must find his way back to his hide out, load, and be gone before sunrise, in order to avoid being captured. Within an hour of following the shoreline, Manta found the right place and immediately loaded the craft with all his precious cargo. The most precious were the fire stones that he secured safely on his person.

The arduous journey began immediately. Pointing the bow of the small vessel toward what he thought was home, Manta rowed away. He uttered a prayer of gratitude to God for having a proper boat, which seemed to glide over the waters with every stroke of the oars. Soon Manta had put much distance between himself and the shore. He rowed throughout the night and by sunrise he could see that the big island was far behind him once again . . .

Soon after, the seas became angered and the winds rose. The rain peppered Manta until his body ached. The waves tossed the little craft as though it were a twig. Manta stopped rowing long enough to lash down his cargo. The boat bobbed violently into each oncoming wave. Manta's attempts to keep the bow into the waves were defeated as the waters filled the little wooden boat, swamping it. He held on to the heavy cargo which hampered the boat's ability to float. Manta let go only long enough to check his body for the fire stones. Fortunately, the craft remained upright even though it was submerged. The clouds instantly swallowed up the light of day. The thunder threatened to break over him and lightening flashed violently, as though it was the devil's search light seeking out the sinner who was abandoned below. Manta huddled in the water-filled punt and prayed for forgiveness for his lack of faith. He prayed not only for his sake, but for the sake of the children.

As the high winds subsided and the light returned to the earth, a solemn calmness came over the seas. The vessel, with a last effort of buoyancy, rose but an inch which broke through the surface. As Manta sat deathly still, he bailed the vessel with his hands while once again being circled by the fishes. With agonizing slowness the water was removed for hours, until the boat finally regained its buoyancy enough to allow Manta to continue rowing. With the wind in his face, he rowed through the night.

As the day dawned, Manta still could not see his island. Fear ripped at his heart as exhaustion ripped at his body. With nothing to eat but salt dried fish, Manta's hunger overrode all other immediate needs. Breaking the seal of a keg, Manta removed a piece of salted fish. Closing his eyes, he ate his first morsel of many during his trip, which took many days at sea in search for his precious island. The storm had swept him out to sea. His source of water was long since used up. His lips, cracked and raw, prevented Manta from eating the salty fish, as the salt burned deep into the flesh and caused his lips to bleed. The burning sun, the lack of water and exposure, took its final toll. Manta collapsed and the boat continued to drift. As long as Manta's mind was alive, he prayed in silence. He practiced once again the children's names until finally he fell into a state of unconsciousness.

No one knew how long it was before Manta was found, but Manta could recall waking up with a thunderous splash of cold water being thrown into his face. Opening his eyes drew fear into his heart, for standing there before his eyes were three white men watching over him. One man held a wet sponge upon his lips, squeezing some of the precious liquid into his mouth. Manta realized that he was aboard another large vessel. He wondered if it were a slave ship; the sponges reminded him of the many wet sponges passed from slave to slave, which provided the only sustenance for hundreds of slaves that had travelled with him in the evil ship.

Manta was powerless at this time to do anything about his lot and lay there for several days while regaining his strength. One day Manta overheard a vicious argument. He soon realized that this altercation was about him. One man insisted that he should be thrown to the sharks. Again

Manta heard that word. Sharks? What is "sharks"? The other voice had more pity and suggested that he should be placed back into his boat and towed behind them. If he could not be sold, he would be cut adrift in the harbour. Who would know? The latter argument won out and Manta was given some dried meat and a jug of water and set adrift behind the tail swell of the great ship.

Manta travelled for many days. The only threats were that of the odd sailor who threatened to cut the life line, and the ever-present devil fish which encircled the little vessel. Manta did make a startling discovery as he heard one of the men call the devil fish "sharks". Finally he had a name for the devil fish and was indeed very thankful that he was not fed to them.

A day or so later produced the most exciting surprise of all, for on the horizon Manta clearly recognized his own beautiful island. How could he escape? He prayed that he would be given the strength and courage to untie the boat and row away unharmed.

Lunging forward, he tugged at the knot which stood between him and his freedom. Finally the knot yielded its grasp and the little boat drifted free. The huge ship, under full sail, apparently did not even notice that the little vessel was detached and continued its journey. Manta rowed as hard as he could toward the island and after an hour or so reached the island, from the northern side. The island was in total silence.

At first Manta's calls for assistance were not answered, and then suddenly many precious little people broke the silence with glee! They too had noticed the ship and took cover, so to avoid being spotted. Soon all were safe once again. Manta's lips were still swollen and raw. His dark skin, now peeling, revealed white blistering spots which covered his shoulders and back. The children could sense that Manta was not well and proceeded with him up the hill to camp. Manta would not rest until all the cargo was secure in the camp. He promised to show them his wonderful find, the fire stones, in the morning. Exhausted he fell asleep.

It was midday when Manta awoke, the children showered him with food and gifts. Immediately after, Manta called all the children together for prayer and thanksgiving. When all the prayers and songs were completed, Manta pulled from his pockets the precious stones. He summoned some to bring dry grass and kindling. When all was prepared a precious drop of the liquid from the small jug was placed on the kindling and Manta, striking
the stones, unleashed their magic. The bulging eyes of the children attested to their amazement as it burst into flame!

Joy and Sorrow

Needless to say the ensuing months were warmer, breakfast was sometimes boiled eggs, meals were cooked, and the stones were in a special place and valued by all as a precious gift from God. The standard of living grew better as the meals improved, but Manta could see that the children grew restless and many had dreams of strange things. As the days passed the children grew ill and soon all were unable to stand. Manta again prayed for forgiveness, as surely this was a curse and God was punishing him because of his disobedience. Once again, Manta's inner man asked for silence and Manta listened intently.

The silence revealed that the children were having a hard time breathing. There, in the silence, was a slight odour wafting through the air. Manta was led to follow his nose which directed him to the barrel of salted fish.

The smell permeated the air when the lid was removed. It had spoiled, probably because of the moisture during the long trip through the storm. Manta emptied the barrel of its contents to find to his horror, many worms crawling out of the flesh of some of the fish. Repulsed at what he had witnessed, he frantically overturned the barrel and destroyed the last of its contents on the ground.

Not knowing what to do next, Manta fell to his knees in prayer and asked God to direct him to the answer to this crisis. The answer was not as easy to believe as Manta wanted.

He wrestled for hours before he forced himself to obey. There before him lay the body of Joseph, lifeless. Manta shook the child violently, crying aloud, his eyes pouring tears onto his cheeks. The grim reality was that the angel of death had taken the child home to glory.

Throwing his all before the alter of God, Manta gave the remaining children a spoon full of the fire-starting oil in the little jug. Soon all were retching and emptied their stomach of the poisons. Manta was pleased to see the response, but his efforts to revive little Joseph were of no avail. The little body lay limp and cold. Manta held him in his arms for hours until he could produce no more tears.

The children laid in their vomit for the entire night. Only the breathing and the foul stench gave notice that the liquid had done some good. Manta could not sleep that night and gazed upon the child several times throughout the night.

He knew that the child's mother was one who was taken to another island. He wondered if the mother was still alive. "Oh God, why me? Why am I given this job . . . no one is supposed to die in de Promise Land. Why, why? If only I obey you Lord, dis would not happen."

Manta covered the face of the child with the leaves of a banana tree and cried himself to sleep.

The next day the children, still weak from their illness, were ushered into the blackest day of their stay on the island, as they dug the shallow grave and thanked God for giving Joseph to them for this time. In anguish they sang, "Swing Low, Sweet Chariot", "Nobody Know De Trouble I Seen", and many other songs of yearning only a child of God could sing. The sound of sand covering the child's bloated stomach would stay with Manta throughout his life.

This tragedy drew doubt for many weeks in the heart of Manta. He found it difficult to forgive himself for the tragic loss.

The children soon recovered physically and mentally, but the death of Joseph, the youngest, drew deep sadness in the hearts of all. He was remembered in prayer everyday.

Although you see me goin' long so,
Oh yes, Lord.
I have my trials here below,
Oh yes, Lord.

Nobody knows the trouble I've seen,
Nobody knows but Jesus.
Nobody know the trouble I've seen,
Glory Hallelujah!

CHAPTER 10

Growth

The vagabond community grew stronger as the years passed. There were good crops of potatoes and plenty of fresh fish. The yellow onions turned into the most beautiful tubular-like white flowers, some of which were transplanted to cover Joseph's grave. The hen lived long enough to produce many eggs. Her gift to the community sometimes caused problems, as she laid only one egg a day, and the question arose as to who would get the egg. Manta solved the problem by collecting the eggs until five were gathered and the group took turns in rotation. It was a sad day when Esta, the hen, was found dead on the beach. Old age overcame her and her contribution to the group's health ended. The children insisted that Esta partake in the crossover ceremony as well. Many a thankful prayer rang forth in the heavens that day for that bird.

It was a year or so later when the next crisis came upon the children. Manta, now considered the spiritual leader, the black Moses, was called upon by twenty frantic children to do something as Molly had fallen from a tree and was dead. Manta rushed to the scene to find, to his dismay a child whose body was twisted, and her face was bloody and scarred. She laid motionless on the ground. Added to Manta's fear as to what to do, was the ever present urging from the children that Manta had the power to save her. Manta's tears and fears turned to anger. "Stop!" he cried, "Who do you think I am?" He collapsed in tears on his knees and sobbed. Defying his pleading to be left alone, the young vagabond choir broke forth in soft song, "Steal Away to Jesus."

Luke, the oldest, the great believer in prayer, broke the circle and entered the ring with Manta. The trio felt the

95

heaviest presence of the Spirit that they had experienced. So much so that Manta covered his face with his hands so as not to look directly into the face of his inner man. Luke righted the broken body as best he could. There was no sign of life. The child's face was even blacker now, lips blue, from the lack of oxygen in her lungs. Manta screamed aloud, "No! No! I have no power to do this, who am I? I am nobody!"

Manta's mind flashed back to the day that he watched his mother die. He heard her words over and over. "You are de one to help de people, you are de Moses."

His memory of little Joseph crowded his thoughts in confusion. If he had not doubted, Joseph would be alive.

Trembling, he reached out his hand, his eyes still closed. The children were still linked together with a bond much greater than slavery as they sang in the presence of God.

Upon touching the girl's forehead a miraculous phenomenon overwhelmed them. The child coughed and out of her mouth came huge amounts of blood. This was the fist sign of life in almost an hour. The children drew their circle of faith closer. Luke broke forth in prayer as the children's songs of faith filled the air, "I Know the Lord Done Laid His Hands on Me."

Manta, feeling so inadequate, could not believe his eyes as the child opened her eyes. As she turned her head, Manta could hear the neck bones snap back into place. Her face soon regained colour. The presence of the Spirit was so strongly about them that Manta rose to his feet, lifted the child from where she lay, and carried her out into water up to his waist. He gently laid her beneath the water, when she surfaced she was full of the Holy Ghost. She sprang to her feet and joined the circle of song. One after another came forth to be baptized in the tide of the Great Flood. Manta felt as though he too was being pulled beneath the water. He gave in to its power and collapsed beneath the flow for several minutes. So long was he under that the children feared he would not surface, and sprang to his aid.

Manta's burdens were lifted, and as he rose up from the sea, he realized that he, too, had received the Holy Ghost. Arm in arm the children silently left the beach. They proceeded up the hill to their camp sanctuary and warmed themselves around the campfire without a word being said. Before too long all lay asleep. As Manta watched his lambs he now knew, once and for always that, yes, he was indeed his brother's keeper.

It was not too long after that, the peace of the sanctuary was disrupted in the dead of the night. A loud crash was heard at sea, loud enough to wake Manta and several others. Seeing nothing in the darkness confused them even more. Splashing and the strangest sound which kept them guessing as to what it was increased their fear. To avoid being seen, Manta doused the last ashes of the fire, in case these noises meant trouble. The vigil lasted throughout the night.

The morning light brought an even greater mystery to the group. Far away in the distance there appeared to be something in the water, which occasionally made a loud splash and gave a horrible bawl. Manta knew this had to be an animal, but what, and why way out there?

Curiosity soon got the better of him. Uprighting the boat, he and Luke set out towards the object and hastily propelled the craft toward the strange scene. Not too far from shore the boat hit a solid object. Turning to investigate, the boys discovered that they had collided with part of a ship. One of the huge cloths attached to a long, thin, log was floating in their path. Manta, sensing that this could mean trouble, scanned the area with bulging eyes. He did not want to alert Luke to the possibility that there could be people who were lost at sea. Manta rowed faster toward the strange object which was their goal. As they drew nearer Manta saw the strangest sight that he had ever encountered. Standing before him on a shallow reef stood a little brown cow! The cow obviously didn't appreciate not being in her own element and displayed her displeasure by jumping violently about. As they approached the beast, Manta could see that the cow was bleeding. Fortunately for her it was low tide. But after all of these years, Manta knew that it was almost the time of day for the Great Flood to get higher. If they were to save her they must do it now. Gathering whatever they could from the wreckage around them, they found plenty of rope and two wooden barrels. As the boys rowed nearer, the cow miraculously grew calmer, so much so that Manta petted her head and calmed her even further.

Gathering the barrels, the boys lashed them firmly, one on each side of the animal, and with rope, strapped them underneath her brisket securely. The plan was to wait until the Great Flood got higher, thus lifting the cow off the reef and then tow her ashore.

All went well until the dreaded devil fish arrived. Luke's eyes were filled with terror as this was the first time that he had seen the terrible killer fish. The boys worked frantically to scare the sharks away. The tide was coming in, the cow, very nervous about the confusion around her, made springing leaps, sometimes lifting the barrels out of the sea. For hours the boys struggled to save her, but Manta noticed that the island was getting further away. This drew fear in Manta's heart. He soon made the decision to cut her loose and return to safety, but Luke would have no part in leaving her and soon convinced Manta to continue the fight.

Then, suddenly the cow gave out a loud, mournful bawl and sprang forward. Manta saw the water turn red in front of her and knew that the worst had happened. The cow, kicking frantically, thrashed about in violent jerks. Manta sprang on to her back and with an oar tried once again to beat away the attackers. Suddenly a sharp pain ripped up his leg. Looking toward it he saw the water rapidly changing colour, but pain was soon overridden by fear. Darkness befell them. Manta was now rowing as fast as he could toward shore and Luke was swiping at the sharks with a rope. The cow was still kicking and thrashing. All at once the sharks gave up their pursuit and soon after the boys could see that the cow's feet had landed on solid sand beneath the water. The barrels were removed immediately and without much hesitation the cow limped ashore. To the boys shock she had but three and a half legs. Remarkably the bleeding had stopped. She hobbled up on the beach and laid down.

Manta, upon examining his own pain, discovered to his amazement that he had lost all of his toes and half of his right foot to the sharks! There was no pain, nor did he bleed. Before retiring, a prayer of thanks was offered.

Next they bandaged the wounds of the cow and Manta. The cow still lay on the beach and did not move throughout the night. The cow's plight drew more attention than Manta's feet. The children showered it with gifts of food which she ate freely. To everyone's surprise the cow did not move while a primitive bandage was applied. The little cow's udder was full of milk which secreted from her teats even as she lay. She drank as much water as the children could bring her. Before long she pulled herself up on her one front leg and using the bandaged hob of the other she stood, much to the children's delight.

It was not until three, maybe four days later that the grim story unfolded as to what had happened. There had been a ship wreck on which the cow must have been a passenger. More horrifying was the body that washed ashore. The terrified screams of Rebecca filled the air as the entire troop raced to the beach to see what was the matter. The body was that of a man. Huge pieces of his upper arm were missing. It was probably torn away by the sharks. He had little hair but he wore a white beard. The children were stunned at such a sight and stood a distance away in silence. Manta, no stranger to death by now, knelt beside the corpse for further inspection.

The body was stiff and cold and Manta would never forget the eyes. The eyes were open and seemed to stare at Manta wherever he moved. The dullness of colour added an even more eerie feeling to this horrific episode. After much prompting, a nervous contingent of pallbearers partly lifted and partly dragged the decomposing body to where all agreed was a suitable burial site. The children, taking turns with the only spade, worked throughout the remainder of the day until, finally, a suitable resting place was prepared.

There were some among them who felt that the body should be flung into the grave and buried without the prayer or the praise of the crossover ceremony as the man was an intruder and a white man. But Manta soon searched his heart and remembered his promise never to hate them, and hushed the negative among them into silent respect.

It was here that Manta realized how marvelously wise his mother truly was. He thought about all the things that he
100

could hate a white man for, but realized that his mother's pleading never to hate, had he disobeyed, would probably draw him to violence and revenge and no doubt would have led to his own death, as it did many others who tried. Nelly knew that if he did not hate the whites, he would have a better chance of survival. Though she was right, Manta realized that not hating took more than doing so. It took a genuine effort to see the good in all men, no matter how small the deed. His mind raced back to the white man that was with Mama Moses and the big Indian in the woods. He searched his mind for other examples but came up short. Dismissing his negativity, he soon returned to his promise to his mother and promptly proceeded with a Christian burial. The children were challenged to truly forgive, and those who could not find it in their hearts to do so had to rededicate their lives to Jesus, because Jesus could forgive his enemies even though they hung him on the cross. Surely we can forgive this white man.

When the final shovel of dirt was thrown, the children returned to the duties of the day. The cow had brought a great gift to the island. It did not take Manta long to master milking once a day. So "Flower" was milked. For many years the three-legged cow supplied the camp with milk. In fact, not so long after her arrival, she blessed the children with a baby. A bull calf which was named "Sampson". Sampson in later years caused quite a commotion on the little island by chasing the children, spreading a deep fear in the hearts of some and deep hatred in the hearts of others.

The great round-up to catch him was even a greater challenge. Attempts to corral him failed as there were little or no trees that produced strong enough wood to properly confine him. The day also came when Flower had yet another baby, this time it was a heifer calf.

The food supply was now becoming scarce due to the livestock competing for the same food supply as the children. The water supply was being threatened as well, as their only source was from the rain which settled into man-made pools which the animals had no respect for and sometimes stepped into in order to drink. Thus the clear, sweet-tasting water was turned to puddles of mud.

After many desperate attempts Sampson was finally caught and tethered to a stout tree. He grew to be so vicious that the children had to bring food and water to him daily. The children now felt less threatened and soon started to adjust with some normality. Discussions as to what to do about their dilemma ranged from killing the bull and eating him, to feeding him to the killer fish by chasing him out to sea. But the children would have no part of that. Many a prayer was raised to the heavens for the mellowing of the temperament of that bovine demon.

The final solution to their serious problem solved itself. One day the children were alerted by the sight of a boat approaching their island, and huddled closely by Manta's side. In Manta's heart he knew it was over. His mind ushered him into what he knew was going to turn the page of yet another chapter in his life . . .

Didn't my Lord deliver Daniel,
Deliver Daniel? Deliver Daniel?
Didn't my Lord deliver Daniel?
Any why not every man?

CHAPTER 11

Deliverance unto . . .

They watched in fear as the boats neared. Manta prayed with the children and called upon his Lord to deliver them from evil. As the boats were pulled ashore, Manta motioned the children to rise. One by one they revealed themselves until all stood visible in open view of the men.

The men silently motioned the children to come forth. The children froze until Manta took the first step. Manta's mind raced for answers as the procession of reluctant castaways slowly descended the hill.

To Manta's surprise the men did not carry guns, but all were armed with spades. There was one man, an elderly man, who dressed strangely. He wore a totally black garment which resembled a woman's dress and around his neck hung a long black braided piece of leather embedded with black beads, at the lower end hung a silver cross. Who was this man? The men appeared to be totally shocked to find anyone on the island, but still no one said a word. The man in the dress opened his arms and embraced an equally confused child of God. The silence was broken by one of the men.

"My God, who would believe it? After all these years."

Another interrupted with "They're not dead! We came here to bury bones."

The man in the dress replied, "And I was sent to perform last rites, but they said it was seven years ago! How did you get here boy?"

"Dey drop us here sir, long time ago." replied Manta.

The priest looked Manta over and cast his eyes upon his feet, "What happened to your foot?"

"Devil fish, sir."

"Devil fish?" queried the priest.

During this time several men were combing the island, astonished to find that there were some twenty-one children, enough potatoes, barrels of salted fish, enough vegetables to feed an army. There were two cows, one with three legs; and one bull, the mighty Sampson, who gave one of the men a frantic chase until he reached the end of his rope.

One came upon little Joseph's grave and called upon another to see it. Manta's mind sped beyond its ability to decipher what these people would do next.

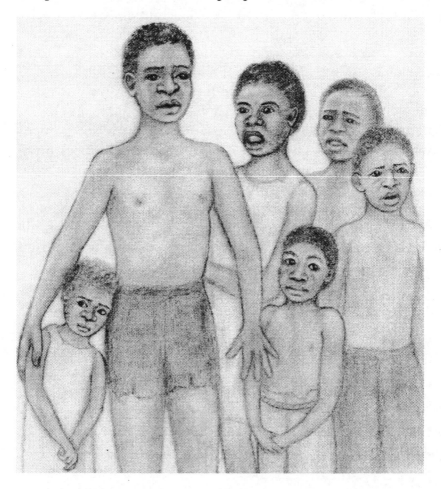

It was obvious that they had come to clean up the island of bones and any other evidence of human existence.

The old man placed an arm upon Manta's shoulder and proceeded to walk slowly on the beach. The children followed them closely. When the priest stopped, so did the group. The old priest carried a look of fear and wonderment. "What am I to do now?" he spoke aloud, "You're all very much alive!"

"Yes sir," replied Manta.

"But how?" queried the priest.

"De Lord dun look after us." Manta replied.

The priest ushered the men together. Manta watched the exchange of words between them. After a brief discussion the children were told to gather their belongings and return to the beach.

No one moved but Manta, he slowly ascended the hill to the camp. There, in his secret hiding place, he removed the fire stones and returned to the beach.

The children were hurriedly loaded into the small boats. When all were on board the oarsman rowed toward the great ship.

The children were silent. Manta's mind raced with thoughts of despair, but somehow he knew it was time to put trust in a higher power as to what the future had in store for them.

As they boarded the ship they were instructed to lie on the deck. Soon the huge sails were inflated with the air of a gentle wind and in silence the great vessel drifted away into yet another adventure into the unknown.

Terrible memories of the first long journey permeated his thoughts. He remembered being made to lie down while being chained to a hundred other souls. He remembered as they placed the flooring planks above them, only inches above his face as the cargo was loaded above, the total darkness, the horrible smell of human excrement, the cries and moans of the dying and even worse, the silence of the dead . . .

As he listened to the white foamy waves beat against the ribs of the ship, Manta's thoughts of the unknown soon replaced the horrors of years past. "No time to mourn the dead," he thought. "The dead are in heaven and they, the living, still have to get there."

As the darkness of the night consumed the light of day, the children succumbed to the excitement and stress of it all and fell asleep.

The noises of the crew, the fluttering of deflated sails, and finally the loud clatter of chain and anchor breaking the surface of the water jarred Manta from his sleep.

Pulling himself to his feet, he could see that they had stopped. The crewmen were securing the vessel to the dock. Manta took a few steps toward the rails to see if he could catch a glimpse of what was surely going to be new surroundings in yet another chapter in his life.

The gangplank thumped loudly as it hit the dock. The children were motioned to leave the ship, but proceeded only after Manta made the first move.

As Manta approached the gangplank his heart thumped in fear when his eyes cast upon the familiarity of the surroundings.

His eyes were cast upon the very village where he had stolen the little row boat with which he had made his last journey to the island!

Soon all were landed on the very dock that Manta had hidden himself under many, many, months ago.

The sight of the children soon attracted an audience and they were being viewed as though the people had never seen anyone of this colour before.

Obviously fascinated by the spectacle, the people gave close inspection; curiosity tempted some to prod the children as though they needed proof that they were in fact flesh and blood.

The man in the long dress reappeared and restored order. The children were led away with a congregation of curious onlookers in close pursuit.

The procession proceeded through the streets of the little village and came to a stop in front of the village stable.

The man in the long dress led the children in and closed the big doors behind him. The smell of hay and fresh manure filled the air. Several horses were stalled, the many sets of harnesses sparkled with silver studding in the reflection of the dim light. Manta scanned the large room. There were several small windows and all of them had curious onlookers peering thorough at them.

The man in the dress tried to comfort the children by offering them fruit and two loaves of fresh bread. The children's eyes gazed toward Manta for approval. At his nod of agreement, the children frantically devoured it within minutes.

The man in the dress left without saying another word. As the doors closed, the children huddled around Manta, waiting for some sort of advice. Manta had none but led the children in prayer.

During the night the only interruption was that of the neigh of horses and Manta's final query to his God, "O Lord what be in de tomorrows!"

The immediate temporal needs of the slaves have always been few. Especially true with this brave troop of souls born into slavery.

A hut, enough clothes in which to keep warm, food and the odd chance to worship, constituted their greatest needs.

With this in mind, Manta comforted them by humming the well known spiritual "I've got a Robe, you got a robe, all God's chillun got a robe."

The tomorrows were soon to be answered. The next day brought with it the affirmation of Manta's worst fears as suddenly the doors burst open and several men dragged the children to their feet. Many broke away from their captors long enough to cling to Manta's legs and waist. The snap of a horse whip drew blood on Manta's face. The children released their grasp on their protector and in peace they left the building.

Outside the children were met by a delegation of well dressed men and many of the towns people. Among them, to Manta's surprise, was a black man, like himself. This man, obviously a servant, stood beside a beautiful black coach with silver fittings.

A man dressed in grey and a lady with the finest of garments were helped down from the coach by the black man, who bowed at the waist while doing so.

The company of dignitaries stood far off in discussion. The man in the dress seemed to do most of the talking, but Manta could not hear the conversation.

Finally the discussion ended. The man dressed in grey stepped forward and the man in the dress raised his arms above his head to motion the people to listen.

Then the man in grey spoke. "As you all know the British Empire abolished slavery many years ago. Today we have an unexpected situation that we must deal with. We have two choices: we can allow these blacks to run loose and God knows what will happen; or we can take them in, feed them, and make them earn their keep. Now, who wants one of these healthy blacks for free?"

Manta soon saw the justification, after all one could not call this slavery if you didn't have to pay for your slave.

Several hands went up and the first person to step forward to claim his prize was met by fierce resistance from the young girl he chose. Finally, two men stepped from the crowd and bodily threw her into the back of a wagon, then jumped in beside her to keep her from escaping as the driver galloped the horses away.

The next person to be chosen was Manta himself. A finely dressed man pointed at him, which instantly drew some objection from the man in the dress. After a brief discussion, the man conceded and chose another.

The man in the dress approached Manta and said, "The Governor has chosen you, you will go with Charles here, and he'll see that you get there." Charlie, a short white man with red hair, though well dressed, did not look the part, it was apparent that he was a labourer of some sort.

All too soon all the children were taken away. A deep sadness ripped through Manta's heart as though he was witnessing the death of his own children. His turn to leave came all too soon. He also met Charlie's temper, which exploded the instant Manta showed the least resistance. Charlie pulled a short chain from the back of the carriage and Manta's right wrist was shackled high up on the back of the carriage. The buggy whip gave command to the two black horses and the long, painful journey began as Manta had to keep pace with the carriage.

The loss of half of Manta's right foot made it impossible for Manta to keep pace for long and he often fell and was dragged along the way. He felt at times as though Charles had forgotten that he was even there. At times the horses were brought to a gallop, causing Manta to pray for hills whereby the horses would be forced to slow down.

The Governor nor his wife did not so much as look behind to investigate the pleading for mercy, as the pain ripped through Manta's body.

At nightfall the coach finally came to a stop in a small village beside the sea. Pain riddled Manta's body. His feet were torn to shreds and bled profusely.

The Governor and his wife disembarked without noticing the broken body, which hung semiconscious by one arm behind the coach.

It did not take long before the black boy became once again the spectacle of scorn, amazement, and abuse.

He was prodded with sticks and the children showered him with stones. He could not hide nor escape their wrath as he remained attached to the coach.

Much later when Charles, the coachman, returned, Manta's persecutors had fled. Manta was beaten to the ground and Charles, with what appeared to be a rare act of compassion, released the shackle and attached it to a lower part of the coach. This made it possible for Manta to at least sit on the ground.

The horses were removed from their traces and taken away. Manta laid in agony as the blood from his wrist flowed freely down to his elbow and saturated the ground beneath him.

Were it not for the rain, which poured throughout the night, he would have fallen into a state of complete unconsciousness.

The slave, though no stranger to pain, had the firm belief that someday the promise that God gave his people that there will be no more sorrow, was exemplified by the saddest story ever told, when Jesus himself drank the cup of human suffering and never said a mumbling word. With this song in his heart, Manta fell into a deep sleep.

They crucified my Lord,
An' He never said a mum-ba-lin' word,
They crucified my Lord,
An' He never said a mum-ba-lin' word,
Not a word, not a word, not a word.

The Victory

The morning exploded with noise and haste as a sharp kick to the ribs instantly drew Manta to his feet. Charlie reshackled him higher up on the back of the carriage and soon the horses were in place in their traces and harnessed. Manta, seeing no hope of obtaining food or water, reached to a bloody puddle of water and with his left hand, scooped a handful of the precious liquid and sopped as best he could a few drops of its moisture.

Soon the procession continued. The horses bolted and the wheels rotated, slowly at first, then as the momentum grew, it forced Manta to once again run to keep up. Every step he took left a trace of blood, leaving him weaker. The weaker he grew, the slower he could run. The lack of blood and energy finally took its toll as Manta collapsed. What happened next and how far the horses dragged him, he did not know. The next light Manta saw was many hours later.

When awakened from his unconsciousness, he was in a dark room no bigger than a closet. In the far distance he could see a dim light, from a small window. When his eyes adjusted, he could see that dawn had not yet come to the smoky grey sky. The light cast a strange dance of movement as the clouds in the heavens slid by the faint outline of the moon.

Manta pulled himself upright and strained his eyes to view his surroundings. Looking down toward his feet he could faintly see that they were bandaged. Grasping the bars he pulled his weak body to a standing position. The cold grey darkness added a strange air of loneliness.

So alone did he feel that he wept in silence. For some reason God surely had deserted him. The scourge of self pity overrode his faith as he tightened his hand angrily around the rusted bars. "Why? Why did you brong me here, dis far, to die as a slave?"

Looking down at his chains, his thought turned toward the children and their plight. Searching his mind for an answer, he found none, digging even deeper as his mind went back to a time when he witnessed a mother who watched her daughter as she was resold into slavery. The flashback brought to mind Mary, the mother of Jesus, as she watched her son on the torture stake. In deep distress, he began to sing aloud,

> "I'm troubled in mind, I'm troubled in mind,
> If Jesus won't help me I's surely will die,
> I been buked and I'se been scorned,
> O, yes, Lord, I'se bin talked about,
> Sure's you're born. Yes, my Lord."

The broken sound of his voice echoed throughout the

dark chambers, song after song rang back to his ears, when suddenly a voice interrupted his melodic tone.

"Boy, who is you?"

Manta slowly raised his head. There before him silhouetted in the light of a flickering lantern, was a woman.

If I'se let yous out o dare, yous ain't goin kill me, is you?"

Manta was too shocked to answer.

"Answer me boy. O I don't let yous out."

"I s'pose to give yous a good scrubbing and make you 'sentable for de Gov'nor. Massa Charlie tell me yous a heathen, Lord knows chawl I'se don like heathens."

"No mam, I no heathen. I'se a Christian, I'se pray everyday, and sing dem spirituals, jes like my mama done to me."

The woman smiled. "Dat good nuf fo me, come odda dare chawl, we's got to clean yous up for the Gov'nor."*

The huge key clanked as it turned the old tumblers in the lock. "Massa Charlie say he gone tame you's cuz you's like a big black lion and you's need tamin', yes sir he did."

The woman proceeded on her way, reluctantly Manta followed through the long corridor until they reached a stairway, which led up toward the same source of light that Manta had witnessed earlier.

The window was barred and as they passed, Manta

* I asked Manta if the Governor she spoke of was truly the Governor of Bermuda at that time. He did not know for sure, as many black folk in those days called their boss 'Governor.'

could see and hear the Great Flood as it crashed against the jagged rocks below him. The cool breeze carried a mist of salt water which gently caressed his face with every thundering crash of the waves against the shore.

Before long the duo entered a room where there was a large wooden tub filled with water. "Take dem rags off, chawl, and git in dat tub."

Manta's only clothes were trousers, not much to

discard. Quickly he entered the water to cover his shyness.

His foot burst into explosive pain the instant it was submerged, which instantly turned the water a crimson red.

The black lady queried, "Chawl, what wrong wit you?"

Manta lifted his foot from the bloody water.

"O my Lord, how dis happened to yo?"

Manta painfully replied, "De devil fish."

"Chawl, de good Lord only know what yo bin through, but I'se better try fix dat befoe t'morrow cuz de Gov'nor, he done want you working by den. If yo not wokken by t'morrow you's gon' be in mo pain den dat."

The bath water Manta soon realized was salt water which added to his agony. The black woman laboured over Manta's wound and applied herbs, oils, and other remedies known only to her. The treatment began to ease the pain as the hours passed. His thirst and hunger was sufficed by a grand meal of cornmeal, bread, and baked beans.

The new clothes complimented the clean body beneath them, and to complete the ensemble was the most welcome sight of all; before him was placed a pair of black, shiny boots. Manta's enthusiasm to try them drew some disappointment as his feet were swollen beyond the size of his beautiful boots.

His mind journeyed back in time to remember his mother, who had carried her prize shoes slung over her shoulders as she walked for months, longing for the day that she could wear them into the Promised Land.

He remembered placing them on her swollen feet as he covered her body with shrubbery, which was to be her grave as he bade her farewell.

The urge to force the shoe over his badly lacerated foot was great, but the pain of it all was even greater.

The procession down the dreary halls once again drew fear in Manta's heart. The musty smell, the wood rot, and the cobwebs gave him an eerie sense of insecurity.

The black lady led the way and once again the big key

secured its victim. Manta's facial expression of helplessness drew an explanation from the black lady.

"De Massa's wife she done think you's goin' rise up and kell all dem in der sleep, so's you'se goin have get use to it."

For some reason it was several days before Manta left the care of the black lady, but Manta thanked God for her influence on the person or persons she convinced that his body needed time to heal.

One day, the person behind the lantern was no longer the kind black lady. The day had come all too soon to meet Charlie, it was a day never to be forgotten in the annals of pain and suffering.

"Starting today you earn your keep, nigger. Get up!"

As they climbed the stairs Charlie cursed the smell of the dark cellar. They passed through the servants eating room and into a long hallway which Manta had never seen, and at the end of the hallway stood the black lady. She smiled as he passed. "Member, chawl, you's jes keep singing dim spirtuls yo' mama done taught you, you's goin' be alright."

Charles glared at her in contempt but said not a word as he pushed Manta toward the door which led outside.

Charles pushed Manta in the direction of the harness room where he once again shackled the confused boy to a bar in the window. The song of the whip echoed throughout the estate as it tore at Manta's back. When the whip finished its deadly strikes, Manta stood motionless with head hung low.

His efforts to restrain his tears were all in vain, as he succumbed to the horrific pain.

As he gritted his teeth to expel his anger, Manta felt a calm come over him like a veil of death, which not only covered his head but also cleansed his mind and heart of hatred.

He wondered if death was the only path to freedom, as pain seemed to be the first and foremost in bondage.

If the whip was the instrument of pain and suffering, what was the instrument of peace and freedom?

114

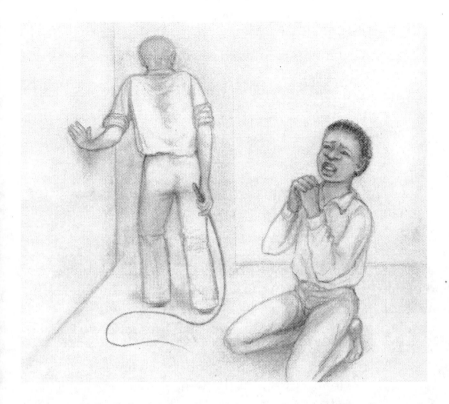

As he searched his mind for answers, he found he knew the answer already.

Only love can conquer pain, suffering and hatred. A man can obtain freedom in his mind and yet be living in bondage.

With all the hurting, Manta started to sing, "Didn't De Lord Deliver Daniel." Charles viewed this as defiance and cracked the whip once again over Manta's raw back.

The day's end was indeed a welcome sight and as darkness grew, Manta had a welcome visitor. The stately, black lady stood over his cell, her presence alone was comforting as so far she was the only friend he had. The ointment she put on his back was soothing and the meal she brought was filling while her conversation was assuring and dispelled the horrible loneliness. She told him that her name was Mabel Tucker. Her parents were both slaves of Mr. Henry Tucker, an important man in government, and lived on the east end of the island. The British abolished slavery in 1832, but her parents continued to work for the Tucker's and also took his name.

The wealth of the Tuckers was immense. Their influence made it possible for Mabel to get the job she now had, which was the Governor's house maid.

"Dey say we's free, but my mama and papa still died a slave," she explained.

The next morning when Charles appeared before Manta, Manta greeted him with a pleasant "Good mornin', Massa."

Charles never said a word, but threw the heavy door open and pulled the boy to his feet, shoving him ahead of him. He kicked Manta which caused him to stumble. In his attempt to stand, a sharp kick to the ribs caused him to fall once again. The beating this morning apparently could not wait until they got to the harness room.

Manta grasped his aching ribs and climbed the stairs once again. He gazed out of the window as he passed. The Great Flood held a special attraction for him today, though he did not quite know why. But the great spectacle inspired him to sing aloud, "Didn't My Lord Deliver Daniel?" This once again brought about more painful examples of Charlie's wrath, but Manta sang anyway.

As he entered the last corridor to leave the building, there stood Mabel, who smiled as they passed and gave her familiar words of encouragement. "Keep singing dem spirtuls you ma taught you, Manta." Her words of encouragement rang throughout the years of stay in the mansion.

The victim truly became the victor, as Manta would sing those spirituals louder with every sting of the whip, Charles' anger weakened as the weeks grew. Every task, no matter how labourious, was greeted with a smile and a song. Charles finally broke down. On one occasion when he was

116

about to use the dreaded whip once again, Manta fell on his knees and openly prayed for Charles.

"O Lord, as you forgive me, the most unworthy one of you chillun, forgive Mr. Charles, who whip me so. And spare him from the pain when you's come to take you chillun home to de promise lan."

Charles recoiled his whip and from that day forward the pain ended.

Mabel constantly warned Manta to beware, as she felt that Charles considered Manta's attitude as mockery toward him.

"Dat man goin' kill you iffen you don't stop enjoying his whompins.", she would tell him.

CHAPTER 12

Family of God

As the years passed, Manta's obsession grew even greater. His desire to free his people drove his hunger for knowledge as to their whereabouts. Mabel, being a person who could not read or write, encourage Manta to study, to learn and to prepare . . .

So a plan was devised among them. The Governor had two children, both in school. These children had a weakness, Mabel's cookies!

Their cravings were soon manipulated into a top secret deal. Cookies for education. Everyday the two children were bribed to teach Manta his ABC's. The arrangement worked fine, until the Governor started to grow leery about how much food was being left on the children's dinner plates.

The plan had to be altered but Mabel did not quite know how. Though the children kept their secret, Mabel was being questioned as to her ability to cook satisfying meals for the Governor's family. She was told to improve the taste or else.

Several new arrangements were tried to no avail. Fruit was not a proper reward. Money had no value to children who had it all. In frustration, Mabel one day sat the children down for the final conquest.

"Chillun," she said, "you Mama say I'se a bad cook 'cause you'se don' eat. You'se don't eat cause o' dem cookies, and I'se need you to keep teaching dat boy."

The new deal involved the making of several new dresses and several unscheduled walks. The cookies continued, but were eaten at school, during the day.

Manta had no slate, but used a charcoal stick on the walls of his closet room.

The journey inland brought about its own awesome splendour and yet the uncertainty of what lay ahead prevented any prolonged exploration.

A half moon struggled against the black clouds which hung low. An eerie sense of panic pervaded Manta's heart, which pounded harder at every step he took to conquer the small mountain of thick, dense, cedar trees.

The temptation to question his Lord grew great as the dew rose up around him like a shroud and enveloped his poorly clad body, until his senses triggered a warning that he needed warmth.

The thick dense bush clawed at his exposed upper body which added to his discomfort. He knew that he must continue, for during the day of meditation, he was promised that this night he would be shown the Promised Land.

The excitement grew with every step. Silence suddenly was broken by a loud clap of thunder which triggered an instant torrent of rain. Lightening ripped across the sky and cracked its awesome whip of fire above him. The wind lashed out its fury at the trees which surrendered the weak branches among them to preserve the strong in their struggle to survive.

"Surely this cannot be the Promised Land. The Lord done tole me dat I know when I see it, cause I would be washed in the water of gold and the Ark of the Lord would mark the place."

He stopped to stand under the protection of the huge leaves of a palm tree, which helped in some small way to shelter his face from the blistering rain.

Suddenly the ground trembled under his feet. The torrents of water which cut its erosive path toward him swept him off his feet and carried him furiously down a muddy path of chaos.

The Promised Land

The fall rendered him unconscious. When he

121

recovered, he lay waist deep in water. To his astonishment upon opening his eyes, he beheld a glorious sight. The morning sun had reflected its beauty in all of its abundance. The water shone like gold. So brilliant was its glow that Manta had to shield his eyes to view it.

Beyond this glorious spectacle of light, he could see the perfect arch of radiant colour, which pulled the final heart string of hope. Yes, this was, indeed, the Promised Land, beyond a doubt.

Standing waist deep in the golden waters, he raised his hands toward heaven and cried aloud in praise to God, for allowing him to view the Promised Land like the chillun of Israel.

The reeds brought to mind the story of Moses, who himself, was set adrift in a basket in the reeds to escape the wicked Pharaoh. Moses' destiny was to lead his people out of bondage and into the Promised Land. He thought of the promises of God who had never failed his people.

Manta climbed the bank to the shore and immediately thanked his Lord for delivering him to such a sacred place.

He prayed for those who, like his mother, had wanted so much to see this place of promised refuge, but were denied.

"Maybe they can see it through me." he thought. An aura of peace surrounded him and once again confirmed that, yes, this was the place where he must now gather and care for his people.

The seclusion, the abundance of food, and the pure water sparked his obsession to recover his flock and bring them home.

As he knelt to pray, he felt the hands of the Lord upon him and he fell into a deep sleep. As he slept Manta was given the entire plan which was to be followed.

Before the children could be recovered, many things must be made ready, starting with Manta's own heart and mind:

1. No longer could he steal anything in order to feed or clothe his people, as it was imperative that no man could hold anything against them. (They must, at all cost, be held blameless);

2. To free his people, he may be called upon to test his word, as anything promised anyone to obtain the freedom of another must be upheld. (Promise no man anything that you cannot or will not give.) Your word must be your bond;

3. Your children will obtain freedom at the sacrifice of your own;

4. He must prepare a place for them first.

The second day was spent in prayer and fasting.

The next day, with fear and trembling, Manta started out across the marsh toward what appeared to be a white mansion. After an hour of walking, Manta was close enough to see that, in fact, his curiosity had brought him not to a mansion, but to a church.

As he drew nearer to it he could see the many gravestones which surrounded it, as if to protect it from the evils of the living.

In its yard was an old sundial which was made of stone with a copper direction wand. There was also a carriage house which housed a strange type of carriage. The old sundial which stood among the graves pointed toward midday. The grass was high among the markers. In some places it obscured the view of them completely.

Manta soon realized that the old church meant that there were people nearby though he had seen no one. His deduction was soon proven true as the sound of a horse-drawn wagon weakened his knees with fear as he threw himself behind the cover of a headstone.

The wagon was pulled by a team of huge, black horses. The driver drew them to a halt beside the carriage house. The sound of the trace chains on the harness brought back memories of his all too recent past. The big horses stood motionless as an old man released them from their act of labour.

Manta watched until the team was stabled before he stepped out from behind his cover. Somehow he felt that he must show himself, so he boldly identified himself as Manta. "I'm Mr. Lambert," replied the old man, "Man, what are you doing here, who are you?"

"I'se a free man," answered Manta proudly.

"Free are you? Well, Mr. Free Man, how would you like a job? I can't pay you much but I can feed you. You can live in my barn."

The offer sounded fitting but living in someone's barn would only bring thoughts of the past. "I won't feel free." Manta thought.

"I'll do it Massa, but I won't stay dere, I don't need yo' food, but I'se work for you everyday iffen I can use yo' tools at night."

The old man looked puzzled, "Will I get them back?"

"Yes sir I'se promise." Already he was giving his word. His word, he knew, he must not break.

"Agreed," replied the old man, "I'll see you here at sun up."

The sound of more horses drew Manta's attention away from the old man. He quickly walked out of sight behind the carriage house and ran toward the marsh.

That night he laid restless beneath his palm leaf shelter, pondering if he had made the right decision.

As the sun rose and cast its first light Manta, eager to start, greeted Mr. Lambert and immediately began the job. Manta found that Mr. Lambert was the grave digger, and yes, his first job was to dig a grave. Manta was no stranger to grave digging. His mind went back to Old Isaac who fell face down in his grave and could not be righted, and to Nelly his mother whose grave was a simple bed of leaves.

The work was hard and long, but at the end of the day the old man kept his promise and Manta took his choice of tools home.

The job lasted many months. During these months, Manta dug many graves and filled many a hole wherein laid one of God's children. Coloureds were not buried here.

The months also provided much progress, enough land was cleared to build a modest home for the children. The digging tools Manta needed were useful, but now he needed other tools for building his home.

He was commanded as to what he must do, and set out to do it. He no longer hid himself and boldly approached people he met as to the whereabouts of the children. He worked on farms, sometimes for months, just to earn the use of tools and building materials. In the evenings he would disappear into the marshlands and laboured throughout the night to utilize the tools to their fullest advantage. Many times he was stoned or driven off. He found that the Lord's plan was working. The offer to work for tools and materials was a great attraction to the farmers who so desperately could use free labour. Before long Manta had bartered enough seed and tools to produce the finest of corn and potatoes. Vegetables were so plentiful that he sold portions and received for the first time in his life payment for his labours. Before long, he had earned six shillings which he treasured.

Manta had built a large wooden shelter with a cooking area and eating room and a sleeping room big enough to bed down his children. What was even more of a miracle, Manta had accomplished all of this in about three years, undetected.

Manta now felt that he was ready to seek out his children, some of which he knew exactly where they were and even on occasion spoke to them and promised that he would return to steal them away when all was ready.

The first recovered was a boy now believed to be sixteen years old, named John Baptist Dennis. John was a frail person whose back was so bent that when he walked he swayed back and forth and his eyes never left the ground. John worked on a farm about a two hour walk from Manta's miracle home. His owners, named Smith, were good people. They fed John well, but made him work without pay and provided no accommodation for the boy other than to sleep with the animals, mostly swine in a drafty old barn. Manta boldly approached the Smiths about securing John's release and made them a promise that if they would let John have his freedom, John would continue to work for free. They would no longer have to feed him, plus Manta himself would give them one whole day of hard labour, free, each month. The Smiths reluctantly agreed. John and Manta worked the day for the Smiths and that evening packed John's meager belongings, which consisted of a pair of old boots which he preferred not to use, a blanket, five potatoes, and an unfinished wood widdling. Then they started the journey home.

When John and Manta arrived, John was astonished

to see what was accomplished. Why, it was at least as good as the pig barn which he had lived in, but the prospect of no pigs was indeed a blessing.

The night fire provided warmth. The glow of the embers seemed to mesmerize the boys, who gazed into its mysteries. What was in store for tomorrow? To Manta this was the first of many who must be brought home. The night was used for preparation. The plan of secrecy was explained to John. The rules were simple, no one must see you enter or leave the marshland, no outsiders must know where they lived, and every promise must be kept. Total honesty must be practiced.

The next day John returned to the Smiths as promised. Manta went forth to gather his flock.

His devotion to keeping his promise to his children that they all would be found and returned to the fold, kept Manta busy for many, many years. And never once did he break his promises to the keepers of his people, some of these promises he kept to the end of his life.

One promise that he made was that he would supply onions to the Zuil family, to replace the production that one of the children would produce if he were still a labourer.

One of his agreements meant that he would supply vegetables to certain families once weekly to repay the loss of their labourer. Another demanded that a fresh supply of fish weekly had to be supplied as ransom for another's freedom. Another required that their cow be milked daily as repayment. Many others required their homes to be cleaned, fruit picked, bread baked, etc.

Yes, Manta knew that legally he did not have to adhere to any of the conditions set out by any man, as slavery on this island had been abolished some fifty-six years before, but he kept his word to his God, as well as to himself. Yes, his word was truly his bond.

The colony soon became known as the Children of Pride.

And the Lord added his blessing five hundred fold.

The marshland had turned into a Garden of Eden.

The Wisdom of Manta

A s the years passed many of the men and women sought employment as maids, farm labourers, fishermen, boat builders, etc.

During these years, Manta made many influential friends. In later years he found that the very land he had squatted on was, in fact, owned by a man by the name of Cox. Mr. Cox lived high above the marsh and had known of and watched the settlement grow for many years, but said not a word.

This man also owned a home on the edge of the marsh. It was a very long house with many rooms. The cellar of the house extended the entire length of the house. On the southern side of the house there were a series of half-moon shaped holes cut into its walls to allow light and air into the cellar. This house was built in 1713 by the Cox family and its cellar was designed to house slaves.

It was in this very house that I, the writer, encountered this awesome man of God, by some twist of fate.

My parents raised the majority of my family in this very house; in fact, I and most of my brothers and sisters were born in this house.

When I was born Manta Grant was already eighty-one years old. My earliest recollection of him was probably when I was five years old. The gentle octogenarian helped me up to a comfortable seat on a bench under the poinciana tree in the front yard which was to become in my fondest of memories, a privileged place of tree learning, where he told me the first of a hundred stories that this tremendous man had to tell.

My entire family was touched by this gentle man, who

humbled himself every night after dinner with a daily act of total unselfishness. Every night he cleaned and polished the entire household's shoes, all sixteen pairs of them.

His day started very early and without fail he could be found under the poinciana calling upon his God for guidance for the day. At age ninety-two he was still the family gardener and toiled in the huge gardens, most times alone.

He nurtured the cassava plants with a vigilance, our family did not go without anything that needed to be grown.

The many animals on the farm were raised under his expert tutelage and care. His knowledge of animals was simply astounding, but his knowledge of mankind was even greater.

The preceding story of his life was told to me by himself and other people who had lived the experience with him.

It is here that I, the writer, would like to make a feeble attempt to portray some of the philosophies and personality of Manta Grant as I remember him.

Manta's stories challenged me to hunger and thirst to hear more. This prompted my desire to learn to read and write, in hopes of recording his life story and his sayings.

Visits to Incubator

Incubator was in its day quite an innovative idea. It was built in the early thirties to house some of the Children of Pride who worked for the Zuil family.

Innovative to the point that it surely must have been one of the first ideas for an apartment block and housed some forty or fifty people. Though it is empty now, I remember how I valued my monthly visits with Manta. Usually one Wednesday, after dinner, we would slip away carrying the usual burden of vegetables, sometimes chickens or rabbits. One by one all his flock was visited. Most waited with anticipation to hear the wisdom and advice that he would offer. Every marriage was discussed and approved or disapproved.

But above all, no matter what the issue, they were left in the hands of the Lord for final approval.

His bag of herbs and potions was greatly appreciated and after looking at all the wounds and scraped knees of the children in each household, all were prayed for.

His beliefs made no exception for gossip and he strongly objected to it. He would say that gossip was the sharpest saw that cuts through the chain links of unity which held our people together, "When dat ole saw cut dem links, we is no longer together, and dat is where a lot o' folks want us to be, separated.

Rain or shine, Incubator was a monthly visit geared to hearing the needs and trials of the month. He used to say that visiting the flock on Wednesday makes the Lord's day a whole mess easier to deal with.

On one occasion I remember all too well, we arrived during a fight between one of the Furbert family and one of the Outerbridges. Manta waded in between these two young men, as though he were a young man himself. It was hard to believe that he was in his nineties. The respect that he carried instantly stopped the fight, broke up the crowd, and cleared the attraction. Both boys were sent home to be visited by him later.

When he got to the Furbert house, all the family was waiting. The entire family heard the message once again on how important it was to keep God's links together. Mrs. Furbert had prepared her belt and was ready to apply the seat-warming discipline to her son's posterior. Manta thought that the iodine that he applied to the boy's wounded chin was enough punishment for the day, as iodine instantly brought on the tears which made the apology to the Outerbridge boy far more believable.

When we arrived at the Outerbridge home, Mr. Outerbridge had already applied the cane to his son's bare backside, which did not seem to fairly deal with the magnitude of justice, as the Outerbridge boy complained that his punishment was greater.

Here the suffering of the master of men was brought forth and a challenge to the young man was laid. "Did the Lord deserve what he got and perhaps the boys should think on the sufferings of Christ." The session ended with a verse or two of the spiritual, "Were You There When They Crucified our Lord?" A genuine peace came over the household. After a cup of tea we left to finish our visitations.

I enjoyed most of all our walks over the mountain to and from Incubator. It gave me time to ask deep questions and hear deep answers, for on one such occasion the deep subject was death.

"Death," he said, "is the beginning of true life and living to those of us who are truly with the Lord. All de suffering and pain that dis old body has seen, all dem tears and failures are all rewarded with life eternal. Death to a true Christian is as good as a cool refreshing drink of water when you's sit in the fields picken' taters on a hot afternoon."

"How do you know?" I asked him.

"Because I've been there," he said, "because I been there when I watch my mama die, dat time I feared death so badly my whole body ached with the pain of it. Den a man inflict so much physical pain on me dat I pleaded wit' the Lord to let me die. Den one day I woke up in a grave with sand and dirt all in my face, and de Lord let me see dat I had a job to do, which was far mo' portant den death or dying, cause less your soul is right you ain't goin' see heaven."

He then led us into singing the spiritual, "I've got a robe, all God's chillun got a robe."

Somehow he had answered my fears toward the question of death for the rest of my life and reminded me that God does not allow anything to happen to his children that He knows we can not handle. The more pain and trials we have in this life should make us appreciate the time when the angel comes to take his people home. To the Christian, death has no sting.

Life and Living

"Dis answer of life cannot be answered until we knows how death is goin' bother us. Now if you's a sinner, death becomes the biggest problem you got. If you's born-again Christian, death's no problem."

"Now if you fear death, you don't enjoy life cause your mind thinks that all you's here for is to wait to die. So de man who fears death looks to the worl' for help and do sinful things to justify who and what he is and develops the idea, even though he's afraid to die, that life has no meaning anyway, so let's have a good time and die when you's can't help it."

To the man in the Lord, even though he is in as much pain and trials as any man, he believes he be here on earth for a reason, and looks to God for reasons to do his best during his short life, to do his part to help his fellow brothers and sisters on earth and to accept death as a part of de great promises the Good Book tell us is goin' hapnin when we get to heaven. So to the Christian living is loving—love is forgiving.

Somehow I have never had to question my purposes for living since.

Hate

I once asked him if he hated the white man.

He replied, "No, I learned from my mama long ago that a man who hates will grow up blaming everything dat happen to him on someone else."

"We's got to stop hating. If we stop hating we stop blaming our problems on those who made us slaves and when we have no one to blame for our condition we starts to grow."

"Hate is the devil's curse on our people cause we spen' so much time figgering out how poor we is because of what the man do to us dat we don't see our seed is dying in the very fields we was killing ourselves to make ready for the very people we hated."

Prayer

"You pray a lot but how do you know that the Lord hears you?"

"Well, when I was your age I wondered the same thing. When I was a captive I prayed cause I was lonely and hurting. I was so lonely that I found myself goin' crazy. I started talking to myself so I fought so hard not to talk to myself, cause with all my problems I did not want anyone to think that I was crazy. Cause no one will trust you then."

"Den I started to dream crazy dreams and wake up wid the sweat just a pouring down my face."

"So I started to pray to my God as to which way to go, which rock to hide under, what food to eat, when to hide, who to talk to, who to run from, and when to show myself. These things sound simple to yous but to me dey was vital as to iffen I live or die. You know all de questions I ask de Lord like dis. Never once did he give me the wrong answer. One wrong move and all would be lost. Many, many, times I ask for food and he gimme it, I ask for clothes, he find me the finest. Ask for a job. One time he gimme so much work dat very near kill me and John Dennis. Old Missa Zuil she has us planting dem onions and packing up dem onions in dem cases like you won't believe. I ask for work but dat was hard, hard work.

An der was a time that I used to call dat ocean out der the great flood. Once I was out der, stuck in a whole mess of trouble with the sharks. I pray to the Lord to help me out o' dis problem and glory be, praise de Lord. Dat old log I was on started floating on something. Dem sharks just skidaddled right on out o' there. The night was pitch black, I could not see if we hit a island or not, but I tell you I decided to put my feet down. I was standing on something black and smooth as a baby's bottom, and it was a moving, as skeered as I was. The Lord tole me to relax.

Next morning when the sun came up I was half asleep. Dis big spout o' water gush up in the air in front of me and skeered de life out o' me. When de blowing stopped I look ahead o' me, der was de island that I wanted. All my chillun was a waiting and dis big black ding jus' dove down an disappeared. All I saw was a big splash of a big tail. You know, sharks don't like messing wid no whale, you know. Yes sir, you want to know if the good Lord answer prayer? He sure do."

Faith

"Don't make sense in wasting the good Lord's time about something you is sure is not goin' happen anyway."

"A man need to have de right tools before he start

136

praying."

"Some people pray for rain before they plant the seed, so the rain come, den dey complain dat dey can't get on the land to plant the seed. Some people expec' the Lord to take de seed out o' the bag an' plant it for 'em too. Faith is the reward afta you done your part. You can't expec' corn to grow if it still in a bag in the cellar.

"Faith is believing that all is goin' to work out after we done our little part to make it work. But that's hard work planting seed."

"Would you rather be 'sponsible for making de seed or planting it?" He replied. "A man of faith start working toward the things he does not know the outcome of. De man of faith prepare for the harvest when de plants is small. He sharpen his sickle and prepare his boxes and tings like dat. De man with no faith waits to prove that he will have a harvest den loses it cause he's not got no sharp tools and no boxes to store dem in. Dis man den curses de Lord when it rains while he's trying to sharpen de tools and get dem boxes ready. One man living his faith is worth ten men preaching about it.

White People

I once asked him what he thought about white people. "Are the white people you talk about human beings?"

"Yes."

"Then I think they are God's chillun like you and me. I've met some who think that they be created by someone else, but they be created by the same God, yes sir. White people, black people, we be better off iffen there be no colours. If we all be human beings den der would be no 'stinction. God said all men is created equal. The good book don't say anything 'bout the colour black or white being special. As human beings we's all special in his eyes cause we's all been made in his image.

137

Our moments together soon became the most treasured of my days.

Many times during our conversations he would fall asleep and I wondered many times if I would lose him before he could tell me all. His stories were all fascinating and many times drew me to tears, especially when he talked about his mother and tears would moisten his old eyes, so that he could not hide the great hurt that he had inside.

His strength obviously came from a higher power which sometimes became confusing to my childish mind. It was very hard for me to understand how he could love a God so much when that God had allowed his mother to die like an animal. It was difficult for me to understand why there was a terrific calm which was constantly with him. He expressed to me over and over that he was not telling me his story so that I could grow up to hate, nor was it for me to take pity on him. (But it was most important that I understand that through it all the love of Christ had to conquer Manta first, before Manta could conquer hatred.

"I never seen a man sold thank God. You see, dey give us away 'cause der was no slavery den, it's not slavery if you give someone away to work for room an food . . . but hallelujah I'se always been a free man. Boy when de Lord took this heart o' mine I was free, and if there be any place I didn't want to be, I was gone. De Lord take dis mind o' mine an trabble round the world. When I wakes up next morning, Charles was still der wid de whip. But I crossed over the body. "Cause I was truly washed in de blood o' de lamb."

He closed his comments by breaking into the negro spiritual, "The Jordan River was chilly and cold, chills de body but not de soul," and once again fell asleep.

The Negro Spiritual

"Dese songs were messages from God jus' like the prophets of old. God talks to us from dese songs. Dese songs

138

saved many souls. Led a lot o'people out of slavery you know. Songs o' de spirit, dats what dey are. Give us hope when we needed it most. Not just any man can sing dem, you know. Yes um, youse got to be filled wid the spirit before you can reach people wid them spirituals."

"Spirituals were our good book long before we could read. Dats how we learned about the Lord in dem days."

"I think I knows dem all."

"I'se remember de boat ride here when we's couldn't even sit up 'casue we were made to lay down side by side wid dem chains on our legs to keep us together. Den dey put dem boards over us, den dey put the barrels and boxes and things on top o' dem so nobody can find us. It was so dark you's couldn't even see yo' hand in yo' face."

"But we still sings dem spirituals as loud as you get. O dat made dem sailors so mad dey shout down dem holes. "Shut up, shut up you niggers o' we kill you." But we keep singing dem songs anyway."

"Dey drop sponges down de hole once a day full o' water and we pass dem around so we could get a drink o' water. Once a day watermelon busted all over de place, taste good doe. But dem sponges after awhile tasted purdy strange cause we could not get up to go to de batroom, we had to go to de batroom in our clothes. De smell was awful strong. One day de smell o' death took over the smell o' human waste. For a week or mo' dis smell took over. We's all guessing who done be taken home to glory.

"One day dey stop de boat, made us hang over de side to clean up. We'se still got chains on, I watched many a soul jes' let go an' sink to de bottom. O dat made dem sailors very mad. Dey found the body of my friend Bertha and many oddas, and dumped dem into de sea. But we still kept singing dem songs of de spirit."

Courting

139

I'm not sure if the candle method of courting was strictly the old man's version of dating or had he followed some guidance of a higher being . . .

However, it appears that after both parents gave their consent, the couple had to publicly disclose to the congregation their intention to date each other. The young couple were brought before the old man by the parents. After a pep talk and a blessing he would present the young couple with two candles about one foot in length. One candle was marked off in six one-inch parts and three two-inch parts, which had to be cut into those dimensions. The first six dates, which incidentally had to be at two week intervals, must last the equivalent in length of one inch of candle. When the candle went out the date was over. The following six months dealt with the utilization of the remaining three two-inch portions of candle which could be used monthly. Again when the two inches of candle were consumed the date was over. The candles were held by the old man and had to be obtained by the couple. Shortly before the date a slight progress report had to be given before the next candle was released. The remaining candle was cut in four equal parts and usually when the last of this candle was used the couple had to give their intentions, which usually led to marriage.

The marriage ceremony was held sacred, as the joining of two of God's children was a serious matter and could not be taken lightly. After a lengthy message, the couple were led to the pond side. The couple removed their shoes and crossed over to the other side, hand in hand.

The crossover was to illustrate the willingness of each to go through good times and hard times together, but most of all it was to remind the couple of their devotion to Christ, which was first and foremost over all the promises they may make to each other.

When the couple reached the other side the celebration began. Gifts of food, money, clothing, etc. was showered on bride and groom, and the banquet, which was put on by the congregation, began.

Church Service

His church had no hymn books, no pianos or organs, no pews, no coloured windows and as a matter of fact he had no building. What they did have was an old spirit-filled man of God, who led his people in the path of righteousness with the simplest of songs, the simplest of faith in God's holy word that anyone could ever know. Their shoes and socks were removed out of reverence for this hallowed and sacred place of worship.

The services always started with a stern reminder of the sacrifice made by God, when he gave his only son to die so that they could all be free. As he believed their slavery was not so much that they were, in fact, taken as slaves; but rather that their greatest slave master was a man's own sinful nature.

Thus every meeting started with songs of remembrance and mourning such as, "They Crucified My Lord", and "Were You There When They Crucified My Lord?" These songs were to remind them that no matter what they had been through, nothing could compare to the suffering of Christ.

The second phase of the meeting dealt with the humbling of oneself before the Master.

The scriptures would remind them that though they

had not suffered as Christ had, they needed constantly to seek his mercy. Luke 18:13, which reads, "And the publican standing afar off would not so much as lift his eyes unto heaven, but smote his breasts saying "God, be merciful to me, a sinner." These verses would lead into spirituals such as "It's me, it's me O Lord, Standing in the need of prayer."

The third phase of the meeting was the call to worship. It was here that the congregation was challenged to leave their burdens at the cross, rededicate their lives to the Lord and to reaffirm their faith, in preparation for the Holy Spirit to come among them.

It was here that anyone who felt he had slipped during the week had a chance to ask forgiveness and to shake hands or hug a brother or sister that he or she may have offended.

When the congregation had all the stress, trials, and trouble of the week publicly confessed, and the new believers acknowledged; then the call to the Holy Spirit rang out in song like, "Swing low, sweet chariot", and "Steal Away To Jesus".

After a rousing invitation of song, anyone in the congregation who wanted to raise their voices in prayer and praise did so. Most prayer was raised for the new converts, asking the Holy Spirit to sanctify their lives. During this time the old man would move over to the pasture's pond, being followed by all the believers.

Here anyone wishing to be baptized was fully submerged in muddy water. Spontaneously this prompted the songs like, "Wade in the Water," and "I Know the Lord Laid His Hands on Me."

The collection, as it was called, was preceded by a stern warning that God loves a cheerful giver. But God did not expect his children to go hungry, and the collection was not expected to stop here. The giving of their love and labour toward their neighbour was far more important than a few shekels in the plate.

They were reminded that the sacrifices they made would be rewarded in Heaven. Thus the congregation would break into songs like, "I got a robe, you got a robe, All God's chillun got a robe," it was not uncommon for an individual to give his collection directly to the person that he or she felt had the most need or whom the Spirit had led the giver to give his or her offering to.

It was common to see people with tears in their eyes, sorrowing for their fellow brothers who were in great need.

Throughout the service the children were constantly reminded of Bible stories and invariably someone would burst into songs about one of the heroes of the Good Book. Songs like, "Joshua Fit de Battle of Jericho", "Go Down Moses" and "Little David, Play on Your Harp." Often, simple illustrations were used to drive the message home to the children about the power of God and his wisdom.

The sermon was geared to telling it like it was. Here the old man would open the word.

He publicly grieved over the awesome responsibility given him to expound the word of God. The most sacred of all tasks was being the shepherd of one of God's precious flocks.

That old man, once a slave, to my knowledge never went to school. No statue was ever raised in his honour, he received no medals, his losses were never compensated and he was never rich in possessions. But he lived with the promise that his reward would one day be found in heaven. On his one hundred and sixth year he passed away, the sweet chariot he often sang about swung low for the last time and carried him to glory.

In the pouring rain we lowered him into the ground, to the powerful rendition of the great spiritual, "Nobody Knows the Trouble I've Seen" in the presence of hundreds who loved and respected him.

His funeral was held as he would have wanted it, in the pasture in the rain. His body was laid to rest in Christ Church Cemetery, Devonshire, Bermuda.

Greater love hath no man than this, that a man lay down his life for his friends - John 15:13.

In this feeble attempt to put down in words the power of God that this old man portrayed, it is my hope that all who read this book will receive some sense of God's Holy Spirit throughout its pages, as I have done while attempting to write them.

To Manta Grant, "Farewell old friend, I'll see you there on that day."

I looked over Jordan and what did I see?
Coming for to carry me home,
A band of angels, coming after me,
Coming for to carry me home.

Swing low, sweet chariot
Coming for to carry me home,
Swing low, sweet chariot,
Coming for to carry me home.

ISBN 141203864-2